FALLEN LOVE

SINFUL TRUTHS BOOK 5

ELLA MILES

FREE BOOKS

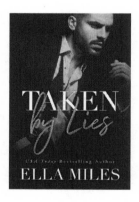

Read **Taken by Lies** for **FREE**! And sign up to get my latest releases, updates, and more goodies here→EllaMiles.com/freebooks

Follow me on **BookBub** to get notified of my new releases and recommendations here→Follow on BookBub Here

Join **Ella's Bellas FB group** to get **Pretend I'm Yours** for **FREE**→Join Ella's Bellas Here

TRUTH OR LIES WORLD

TRUTH OR LIES SERIES:

SINFUL TRUTHS SERIES:

PROLOGUE

"I KNOW," ZEKE SAYS.

Those words haunt me. They dig deep into my heart, piercing my very soul. His words offer me everything I need and nothing I deserve.

"I know, Siren. I know," he repeats again, stepping out of the darkness and into my bedroom aboard the yacht. The moonlight illuminates his face.

My bottom lip trembles. My eyes are watery, but I refuse to cry—I can't cry. Not now. Not after everything we've been through. I won't shed any more damn tears.

Zeke takes a step forward, and my heart wrenches. My pulse is in my throat.

His presence makes me tense. I don't know how to feel about Zeke anymore. His hardened eyes are lost; he doesn't know how to feel about me either.

I look down, twisting the ring Zeke gave me. A ring that represents forever.

A forever we will never have. A forever we both surrendered.

Zeke takes my hand, and I spot his matching ring. A

ring that tells the world he's my husband. He's taken. He's mine.

If only those words were true.

"Siren—"

"No," I snap. I can't talk. I can't speak reason. I can't listen to him explain why things ended the way they did. I don't want to hear that he still loves me. Sometimes, love isn't enough. It isn't enough to survive on.

We need more than love. We need air and water and food. We need trust and truth.

We've both sinned too many times.

We've shed too much blood.

There is no coming back from what we've done.

We've wrecked more than just our love. We've hurt every person who has come into our lives.

Every.

Single.

One.

We are alone now. But not together.

Together we destroy. We ruin. Our love destroyed everyone else we love.

Our love has to end. We can't keep being selfish. We can't keep hurting others. We can't keep sacrificing everything to save the other.

I squeeze my eyes shut, doing everything to keep my tears in—keep my pain in.

"I'm sorry," I say. Sorry that I'm crying. Sorry that I hurt you—hurt them. Sorry that I saved you. Life would have been so much easier had I let Zeke die, had I finished my vow to Julian and then vanished myself.

Instead, I was selfish. I saved a man, knowing our love would destroy everything.

"I'm not," Zeke says, pulling on my hand until I'm

standing in front of him.

Face to face, hands gripping each other, knowing this is the last time we will touch. The last time we will be in the same room together. *The last time...*

"Our love was never meant to last forever," Zeke says, his own tears dripping down onto our joined hands.

"But we promised. We vowed. We loved—forever," I say, my words broken and painful.

"We kept those promises," Zeke says.

I stare at him. Feeling more love than I've ever felt for another human being. More love than I knew was possible to love another man.

"I'm sorry," I say. I grab his neck, my hand fisting his hair, and I pull him down into one last desperate kiss. A kiss to top all kisses. A kiss to survive on for the rest of my life.

Zeke's lips remain closed at first. From shock. From trying to guard his heart. From trying to protect me. He thinks our departure will be harder if we kiss.

I don't give a damn about what's hard or easy.

I love Zeke Kane with all of my heart. I will never love again like I do now. *Never.*

This is it for me. This is it.

One more kiss.

That's what I need to take with me.

It doesn't take much to part Zeke's lips. My tongue is suddenly inside his, feeling alive again for the first time in weeks. I'm floating on a cloud and doing battle at the same time. That's what it's like kissing Zeke.

Zeke's hands grab my hips, holding me tightly against him until I feel every inch of his hardness. I memorize it all. Everything about him becomes ingrained in my memory, pushing all other memories out until I remember this moment, forever.

I remember the way Zeke feels pushed against me. How hard and strong and protective he feels.

Another snap remembers how his wet lips shoot tingles of electricity through my body. How his tongue on my tongue hits me deep to my core.

I will never forget how his hands hold me like he can't ever let me go.

But then Zeke does let me go.

He ends the kiss, effectively ending us.

We both take a step back; it's the hardest step either of us has ever taken, but it's necessary.

We both know what comes next. We both know our future. We both know this is the last time we will ever be together.

We both touch our rings.

Zeke walks out the door, never to return. I'm alone.

Zeke's gone.

The love of my life is gone.

We promised forever.

What a forever it was.

I don't regret it.

Even if I should regret it, at least for the sake of those who were hurt by our love.

I hoped our forever would last longer, but from the moment it started, we were always destined to end. We wouldn't last a lifetime. We wouldn't have kids and grow old together.

I stare at the engraving on my ring.

I promise...forever.

Zeke kept his forever promise.

Our forever just ended sooner than we could have ever imagined. Love saved us, and in the end, it destroyed everyone we love.

1

SIREN

DEATH IS ONLY THE BEGINNING.

Isn't that the saying?

Maybe that's true for some, but it's not what I've experienced. Death is definitely an end. An end that may lead to a new beginning, if those who are left are able to start again.

But sometimes death is just the end. Sometimes death breaks those who are left so deeply, and there is no coming back. There is no starting over. There's just nothing left to do but wait for death to take you as well.

Watching Lucy die in my arms was the hardest death I've had to endure. I thought she was my enemy. I thought of her as the villain. Watching her sacrifice herself, with a cure in her grasp, was the most selfless thing I've ever witnessed.

She died protecting us all because the cure her mother created also happens to be a contagious cancer that could wipe out continents. If any of our enemies got ahold of it— Julian, Bishop, anyone—they could use it to control the entire planet.

Lucy was the only thing preventing them from getting

what they wanted. Lucy protected it. And Zeke protected her. And I protected Zeke. In a way, we are all connected. We are all the reason Julian and Bishop don't have the viles, the research, the key to controlling the world.

"Promise me," Lucy says, as she lays in my arms.

I suck back tears. Lucy isn't crying. I'm not going to let the last thing she sees be my blubbering face.

"I promise," I say, even though I'm afraid I will never be able to keep it. It's a huge promise I just made. A promise that requires sinning and lying to a lot of people, something I've only just managed to be able to do.

Finally, I can't help it. A tear pools in the corner of my eye, threatening to reveal the pain and fear I'm feeling inside as I hold Lucy in my arms, laying out on the grass in whatever country we were taken to. We're looking out at a beautiful lake, thousands of stars shine overhead, and the moon makes the night sky seem lighter than I've ever seen it.

Lucy finds my hand. I hold it, and she smiles up at me.

"Don't be sad for me," Lucy says, raising her frail hand up to try and wipe my tear. The one tear rolls down my cheek with the speed of a freight train. And then all of my tears are cascading down my cheek.

"How can I not? This shouldn't have happened. You should have had more time. I should have made sure Zeke chose you, not Kai. I should have—"

Lucy coughs. I stroke her back, trying to get more oxygen into her lungs, even though I know her time is dwindling.

"No, I didn't want Zeke to have the burden of watching me die. Someone who loved you, like we loved each other at one point in our life, shouldn't have to be here to see me like this. I want him to remember me as I was, not like this."

I nod, understanding. When my time is up, I hope Zeke isn't there. I couldn't stand for him to be there. I don't want him to ever have to remember me as anything but the woman who loved him deeper than he's ever been loved.

I squeeze her hand tighter. "I'm happy to be here."

Lucy smiles. "Who wouldn't want to watch their competition for the man they love die?" She teases.

I hug her tighter in my lap. "If you had wanted Zeke, you would have won. I can't think of a more incredible woman."

She nods. "I know. But I fell in love with Palmer. I don't want you to think Zeke was the love of my life; he wasn't. Palmer was. Zeke is just an incredible best friend."

"I know."

"Tell me about Palmer," I say.

Lucy does; she tells me everything. Without a doubt, Palmer was Lucy's love. As much as it might have hurt Palmer to have to watch the woman she loves die, she should have been the one here.

"Palmer," Lucy says, looking up at me. She's been out of it for the last hour, hallucinating and barely catching her breath. Her pulse is weak, her face is sweaty, and I swear she only takes a breath every minute or so.

"Yes?" I ask, blinking back my tears. I can be Palmer. I can love her in her last moments on this earth.

"I love you," Lucy says.

"I love you, too," I say back. I don't have to lie. I love Lucy. Maybe I'm not in love with her. But damn, do I love her strength, her courage, her selflessness. It's the most beautiful thing I've ever seen.

I kiss her on the cheek.

I watch Lucy take her last breath. I watch her eyes close. I watch her heart thump one last time, and then she's just...*gone*.

I've seen death.

I've taken lives before.

I've killed.

But I've never seen anything so peaceful as Lucy's death. I hold her body in my arms for a few minutes. A crack of thunder startles me back into reality.

I stare up at the sky, and I see clouds rolling in. The storm had been waiting until Lucy took her last breath, allowing her final few minutes on this earth to be filled with beautiful landscape.

I gently roll Lucy off my lap and stand to gather wildflowers nearby. I form a bouquet and rest it in her hands. Maybe I should have negotiated with Julian and Bishop to take her body back for a proper burial, but I don't think Lucy would have wanted that. She would have wanted to feel free, not buried deep in the ground.

I carry her body to the edge of the lake and softly push her floating body out into the water as the storm rolls in. She looks like an angel before she disappears under the water, the pouring rain forcing her down.

I'm thankful for the rain; it hides my tears as I hear Julian Reed approach and turn to face him. I wish I had more time to mourn Lucy, but there's work to be done to keep my promise to her.

"So, you won? You get to have control of me?" I ask.

"There wasn't anything to win. I'm in charge. Bishop works for me, just like you. He will continue his work training your mind later, but first, we had a deal," Julian says, holding his hand out to me.

Julian is wearing dark suit pants, with a rain jacket over it. He looks put together and proper, even out here in the middle of nowhere. Even as the rain pours down, he's unfazed.

I look up into his eyes, and I see what he wants. It's what he's always wanted—*me.*

I swallow my pride. I push down the desire to punch him in the balls. I made a deal with the devil. I agreed to give him myself in exchange for making sure Lucy died with dignity and love. I don't regret it, and I won't renege on my end of the deal.

I made a promise. I'll keep it.

I always have. That's the main thing Zeke and I both agree on. We keep our promises. If we don't have that, then we've lost our identities.

So I take Julian's hand, surrendering myself to him. I pray that whatever was keeping Zeke away before has been defeated, because I need him to come. I need him to save me, even though I've told him not to before. I told him I'm not worth saving; I don't want him to save me.

I've never wanted Zeke to save me, especially from Julian, because every time Zeke saves me, it risks Zeke finding out the truth.

But without Zeke, I won't survive this time. This time, I need him. This time I need Zeke to save me...

2

ZEKE

MY SHOULDERS ARE THROBBING AND TENSE, THAT'S THE FIRST thing I notice before I even open my eyes. My left hand is numb, that's the second.

I open my eyes. A dizziness and splitting headache hit me next.

I blink. I've dealt with all of this before, it's nothing new. I'm not going to let an injured arm and a headache keep me from doing my job. My job is simple: protect those I love.

I quickly take in my situation in a matter of seconds. My wrists are tied, stretching me wide over my head in a V. My left hand is crushed, which is why I can't feel it. And my shoulders are sore from being stretched. I'm not wearing a shirt, and sweat is falling down my neck and forehead.

Drugs are still pulsing through my system—that's why I'm sweaty and my head is so foggy. My ankles are also tied with thick chains bolted to the floor.

I kick, testing the strength of the metal—it's heavy-duty. It's going to take a lot of effort to break free, especially in my state.

I survey the room as well. I'm underground, most likely

in a basement from the lack of windows and unfinished floors. There is a lamp in the corner, but otherwise, I'm in the dark.

But I'm not alone.

I can hear the breathing of another person; the breath speeds as the person realizes I'm awake. He or she can now question and torture me.

My brain quickly puts all the pieces together. I was in Julian's house. I was going to get Siren and Lucy back. I went down, into a tunnel, and then a crash...

A boulder trapped me in the tunnel. A woman stepped forward from the darkness.

I look up, and the same woman is standing in front of me now.

She's a small woman, much smaller than Siren. She's probably five foot nothing. Her muscles are thin and long, not like the bulky brutes that normally inhabit my world. It's clear she doesn't usually carry a gun or weapon. She has no skills in martial arts or fighting. I can see it all in the way she carries herself. In fact, she looks like she's about to cry as she looks at me.

Her watering eyes trigger my own suffering. Lucy is dying, and I'm not there to comfort her. Siren is probably being tortured or raped, and I'm not there to protect her.

Please, god, let Beckett, or Enzo, or Kai...let one of them be there to save her. Please. I'll never ask for anything again. I just got Siren. She said yes to marrying me, yes to forever. She said yes.

Now, she's gone.

I failed her.

I promised I would come back when I saved Kai over her and Lucy. I promised. But I failed.

"How long?" I croak, but my voice answers for me. I've

been out of it for days, most likely. My throat wouldn't get this dry, my shoulders wouldn't throb this badly, and my hand would still feel the pain if it had only been a few hours.

"Three days," the woman answers me.

My eyes fly open again, and my arms and legs struggle against the chains as I roar in agony.

Three.

Fucking.

Days.

So much could happen in that amount of time. Lucy could have died. And Siren...

God, I can't think of what Julian or Bishop could have done to her in that amount of time. After I got Siren back from Bishop, she was barely able to keep it together. This time...I have no idea if Siren will be the same woman or not. If she'll ever forgive me for failing her.

I'll never forgive myself.

The woman pulls out a cigarette and lights it. "You can struggle against those chains all you want, but you won't get free."

She puffs out some smoke, and I notice her hand shaking. Her eyes are puffy, like she's been crying all three days I've been unconscious. The nicotine entering her system seems to be the only thing keeping her alive.

"Who are you?" I ask, not sure if she'll answer me. She did answer my last question.

"You don't remember?"

She sucks on her cigarette again. I think back, trying to remember if she told me a name.

"I'm Palmer," she says casually.

"What do you want?" I ask. It's obvious this isn't her world. She's not the type with experience kidnapping and torturing someone. I doubt she's ever killed anyone before. Her manicured nails and general frailness tell me that she probably has never even held a gun before. She belongs anywhere except in this basement.

Most likely, she had loads of help to get me here. She's too small to lift my body. I listen carefully, and I hear the creak of a footstep on the floor above. She had help. I don't even know if she is in charge.

"Nothing you can give me," she steps forward, the color returning to her cheeks, but her pain never leaving her eyes.

"Palmer, I don't know what trouble you are in, but I can help you. I don't care who your enemies are. Let me go, let me save someone I love, and I will do everything I can to help you and protect you. I promise." Palmer has to be in trouble. Maybe she's a drug addict. I look at her arms and see no needle marks. Her skin looks healthy, not the yellow-greenish color of most addicts. And her head seems clear.

She's just in pain—incredible, unmoving pain.

"You think you can help me?"

I nod.

She shakes her head. "I've known you for a long time, Zeke Kane. I was told you are a protector, a selfless savior, but it seems to me that you have a hero complex."

I frown, not sure who she knows that has talked about me. None of my friends would say anything about me to a complete stranger.

"Haven't figured it out yet?" Her voice lifts, getting stronger as her pain spreads through her veins into every crevice of her body. I can see it move inside her, her torture turning to anger.

"Who are you? What do you want, Palmer?" I keep my voice calm, hoping it will relax her.

"I want the love of my life back!" Her voice is loud and echos throughout the room.

I still. My heart catches, and my breath pauses. I'm afraid I know the answer—why I'm here. And I don't know how to convince a person who has lost everything to let me go so I can get the only thing in my life back that matters—Siren.

"I want Lucy back," Palmer says, her hand shaking as she grips the cigarette like it's her lifeline. The tears fall anyway.

"What happened to Lucy?" I ask, needing her to keep talking. To get it all out and not break down. I try testing the chains again, but I won't be able to get free without a lot of effort and strength. Strength I don't have at the moment.

"She's dead! That's what happened. She's dead, and I couldn't save her!" Palmer screams, but it's not the volume that gets me. It's the heartbreak.

I feel it—Lucy's dead. Palmer isn't the only one who failed her; I failed Lucy too.

My tears blur my eyes. I lost one of my best friends, a woman I loved. *Did I choose wrong? Should I have saved Lucy instead of Kai?*

No, I shouldn't have chosen at all. I should have found a way to save them all.

"I'm so sorry. I loved Lucy too. I—"

"No, you don't get to speak. You had your chance to save her and you failed," Palmer shakes her cigarette at me.

I close my mouth. No words can bring back Lucy.

"I tried to use you to bargain with them. I tried to trade you for Lucy, but they wouldn't trade."

My eyes darken. They don't want Lucy—they want Siren. They want what Lucy was protecting. What I was protecting.

"Let me go, and I'll kill them. I'll avenge Lucy's death. I'll kill every single person responsible for her death."

Palmer shakes her head. "You're the reason she's dead, not them."

I frown, not following her logic. She's mourning a woman she loves. She hasn't said it, but she doesn't have to. She loved Lucy. I have no doubt Lucy loved her back.

Lucy loved who she loved—man or woman, it made no difference to her. Palmer wouldn't be hurting so much if Lucy didn't love her back.

"Lucy was dying. She had cancer. The treatments stopped working. I stood by her side. I want to the chemo. I loved her through it all. She told me she was cured. She told me she didn't love me anymore. It was all lies."

She sucks on the cigarette, gaining strength from it.

"She wasn't cured. She was sick. She was dying. The chemo wasn't enough. But what her mother created was strong enough."

"You don't know that."

"Don't I? She had the cure, and she wouldn't take it. Even for me." Tears sting her eyes again.

Palmer looks at me with so much damn pain. "She wouldn't take the cure because of you. She loved you. She wanted to protect you. She knew that opening that box would save her life, but it would risk yours—along with everyone else's on this planet. It wasn't just the cure; it was a curse upon this world."

Palmer's head falls. "It was because of her love for you that she wouldn't save herself."

"No," I whisper.

Palmer's head slowly lifts, until she's looking at me. "Lucy loved you more than she did me."

"No, she wasn't thinking about me. She saved the world. If our enemies got it, they would destroy us all."

"Stop lying! She loved you more. She was protecting you. She died protecting you."

Palmer is in my face now, her anger pulsing off her body, her breath hot as fire, and her eyes bulging with rage.

"Let me help you," I say.

She smiles. "Oh, you'll help me. You'll help me deal with this pain." She pounds her hand against her chest, where I know she's hurting.

"You'll help me by giving me an outlet for my anger. You will feel everything I feel, because you took her from me. And when I'm finished, you will tell me where the cure is."

"Palmer, I know you are in pain. That won't go away easily, but you need help. Let me help you. Torturing me won't help. I'm built to withstand torture. I won't break. I've never broke. You aren't experienced with torturing someone. You aren't a devil. You're not a monster. Don't turn into one. Lucy wouldn't want that."

Palmer steps back, and I see the pain turning into full-on rage behind her blue eyes.

"You don't think I can break you?" Her nostrils flare. "That's only because you've never felt torture from someone who has lost someone they love. You've never felt the pain of a person who has nothing left to live for. I lost everything."

"If you keep me here, I'll have nothing to live for either. We will just be two people locked in an endless battle of pain."

She steps closer to me again, calm and confident. Her calmness scares me. I don't cower for me. I can handle the physical pain she's about to inflict. It terrifies me because every second I'm here is a second Siren is at risk.

I can't save Lucy.

But I can still save Siren.

"This is for Lucy." Palmer pushes the cigarette into my skin over my heart.

I don't react to the pain. I don't feel it. All I feel is Siren.

"This is going to be fun. You're strong. You have your own love you are holding onto. I'm going to enjoy taking her from you."

3

SIREN

I EXPECT TO BE BROUGHT INTO A DUNGEON. A ROOM WITH ropes and chains to bind me, to prevent me from fighting, so Julian Reed can do what he wants with my body.

I expect darkness and pain. I expect him to rip my legs apart and push himself inside.

Instead, Julian holds my hand like we are lovers as he leads me into the large tent-like house in the middle of the African savannah. He leads me past his men. Past Bishop. Past everyone. Until we reach the room at the far end.

When we step inside, it's nothing like the dungeon it should be. This room isn't a cage. This room is awe-inspiring.

Large windows cover two of the walls and the ceiling, giving a perfect view of the starry night and storm clouds rolling in. The floor is white and luxurious, like a cloud beneath our feet. Beautiful candles are lit in one corner of the room, providing romantic lighting. Champagne and strawberries chill on the other side of the room.

This room is meant for honeymooners, for couples cele-brating special anniversaries. This room isn't meant for a man to take what he wants from a woman without her consent. This room can't handle what is going through Julian's head right now. It can't take in the dangerous thoughts.

This room is pure. It's beautiful. It's romantic. None of the things that Julian wants. *So why did he choose this room?*

If all Julian wanted to do was rape me, he would have done it years ago. He wants more. He wants me to surrender to him. He wants me to be his.

My lips tighten, and my heart thumps carefully in my chest, looking for an escape route. Julian can want me to be his all he wants. He can rape and torture me for years in this perfect room, but I will never be his. Even if I wanted to be —I'm Zeke's. I gave Zeke Kane everything, and I can never get my heart back.

"What do you think?" Julian asks, his voice husky and dripping with hunger.

"Pretty. It doesn't suit you," I say.

He brings our connected hands up to his lips, and he kisses the back of my hand before he sucks in a deep breath, taking in my scent.

"You smell like wildflowers," he says.

"I smell like mud and rainwater."

He kisses my hand again, and I jerk it away on instinct. I can't stand his lips touching me. *How am I going to let him do anything else to me?*

I'm not.

I take a step away from Julian, expecting this to be the moment where he grabs me and tries to use his force to fuck me. The moment where he snaps his fingers and guards come running in to pin me down.

I'm ready. I don't have any weapons, but I don't need them. I only need the desire to avenge Lucy's death. The desire to save myself. The pull to Zeke, a man who gave me a ring, and promised me forever.

"Relax, Aria. I'm not going to hurt you," Julian says, his voice purring.

I scoff. "You've already hurt me by kidnapping me. By making the man I love choose between the women he loves."

"I thought he would choose you. I really did." Julian walks over to the champagne, pops the cork, and then pours two glasses.

I watch him from across the room, careful to avoid what is sitting in the middle of the room. I refuse to look at it. If I do, the situation will become real, the fear will rise in my chest, fight or flight will kick in.

I won't run; I'll fight. I'll have to fight every man in the house to escape. I could win, but I could also end up dead. Something I promised Zeke wouldn't happen.

I shouldn't fight. I should be smart. I should manipulate Julian into letting me go. I'm just not sure how to do that yet.

Julian walks back to me as my eyes cut to the door behind me.

"It's a metal door. Soundproof. Bulletproof. And I'm the only one who can open it," Julian says, handing me a glass of champagne.

"What do you mean, you are the only one who can open it?"

"Test it."

I reach behind me and push on the door—nothing.

Julian pulls out his phone. "Duncan, try to open the door to my room." Julian ends the call, and we hear a faint sound as a man pushes on the door.

Nothing.

"As I was saying, this is my own little piece of heaven. I brought you here because I knew you would love it. It's beautiful and enchanting, and I'm the only person who has ever been in this room, until you."

I raise an eyebrow. "I know you, Julian. You like nice things, but nothing this beautiful. This room wasn't built for you."

Julian chuckles. "I love how well you know me, Aria. You're right. This room is far too feminine and romantic for my likes, but it's perfect for the woman I love."

He holds out his glass and waits for me to do the same. My hand shakes as I raise my glass in the air. My throat tightens, trying to suffocate me to save me. In my head, I already know what's going to happen next. I know, and I can't stop it.

No, I could stop it, I just won't. The cost would be too great.

"To the woman I love finally finding the man of her dreams."

He clinks his glass against mine, the ring of the crystal hits my ears like a sharp knife to my eardrums. It continues to ring in my ears long after the sound has stopped.

Julian sips his champagne. My weak hand drops my glass to the floor, shattering it into hundreds of tiny pieces.

"Oh, my love, you're shaking. I knew I should have gotten you inside before you became soaked by the rain-storm. Here, let me warm you up."

Julian leans forward, his hand tucking my soaking wet hair behind my hear and gripping my neck in a move all men do when they are trying to comfort a woman before going into a kiss. But there is nothing comforting about his touch. There is nothing welcome about his kiss.

I lean back, just enough for him to notice.

"We had a deal," Julian says in a soothing voice, like he

knows he doesn't even have to raise his voice in order to get me to do what he wants.

He's right. We did have a deal. I promised to surrender myself if he let Lucy spend her last moments in my arms, in peace. A promise is a promise. I don't regret it at all, for Lucy's sake.

I also promised to tell them where Lucy's secret is, the box containing the cure and curse, not that I have a clue. But Julian is too focused on fucking me to ask about Lucy's box.

So this time, when his lips move toward mine, I don't move. I literally don't move. I'm stiller than a statue. I don't breathe. I don't twitch. I don't grimace. I swear my heart, brain, and nerves shut down so I don't feel a damn thing when his lips brush over mine.

I feel nothing, but my damn eyes see everything. I see him lean in. I see his tongue lick over his lips, moistening them in anticipation of our kiss. I see his eyes close, and I hear his soft moan as he kisses me.

I see the shit-eating grin on his face when he ends the kiss a few seconds later.

Fuck, what have I gotten myself into? I promised I would surrender to him, and he's not going to stop with a kiss. The kiss is nothing compared to the thoughts in his head. I won't be able to survive everything he plans on doing.

"That's not surrendering, Siren. You promised to be mine. You promised to give me everything. That was like kissing a corpse. When I kiss you, you're supposed to kiss me back," Julian says, stroking my neck with his thumb like he has a claim to me.

"That wasn't part of our deal. Surrendering and giving you everything is not the same thing," I say, taking a step back again.

His hand drops, and I'm free for another second.

"You aren't one to back down on a deal." He raises his brow, and his smirk returns to his disgusting, vile face.

I surrendered myself to save Lucy.

But I gave everything to protect Zeke. Zeke will never know why. He will never forgive me, either.

I twist the ring on my right hand. A ring I doubt will ever move to my left. It would be a sin. I can't give myself to Zeke, not fully, not in the way I want and he deserves. Not without risking everything.

Surrender and live—keep my promise that I traded to give Lucy a peaceful end.

Fight and die—ruining the promise I made to Zeke to stay alive. To let him come save me.

I'm fucked either way.

"I surrender," I say, keeping my promise and ensuring I live just a little longer. But knowing that by giving myself to this monster, I'll probably want to die.

4

ZEKE

PALMER IS PISSED.

She's full of rage.

It emanates off her in waves. Her wrath has confiscated every corner of her body. Every nerve. Every blood vessel. Every organ is consumed with her anger.

When she pushes the cigarette butt into my skin, it's not just the pain of the searing fire that I feel, it's her anger. It's impossible not to absorb it. She's shoving her anger into the space between us.

Anger—it's such a complicated emotion. You can be angry for so many reasons. You can choose to be angry. You can be angry because you think life has dealt you an unfair hand. Angry because someone betrayed you. Angry because someone is preventing you from getting something you want.

Palmer isn't angry for any of those reasons. She's angry because it hides her pain. She's lost the woman she loves, the only person who matters to her, and now she's blaming me for her loss.

I understand.

I feel the same way. I feel the pain at the loss of my friend, Lucy. If someone had hurt Siren, killed her, I would kill anyone who could have prevented her death, because anger gives you more control than pain and fear does.

Anger gives you a reason to take action. To do something to feel in control.

Pain leads to mourning. And while it can heal you, mourning doesn't let you feel in control. Mourning is letting yourself feel the loss of the person you love; it's letting it consume you. It's not moving on, but it's accepting what happened.

Palmer isn't ready to mourn. The pain would overwhelm her. But she can deal with her anger. And I'm going to be the one who feels all of her fury.

"You're going to have to do better than that," I say as she pushes the end of the cigarette into a second spot on my skin. I don't flinch. I don't feel anything physical, just the hot pulse of her rage.

I don't let her anger in. That's not how I'm going to win. I could get angry that she's preventing me from rescuing Siren. I could let that anger build inside me and turn it into strength to get free of these heavy chains. I could use that rage to take out the dozens of men on guard us above. I could use it to find a way to hunt Siren down and save her.

But it would require me to kill Palmer in the process, something I can't do. I owe it to Lucy. Lucy left Palmer because she loved her and didn't want her to watch her die. She didn't want Palmer to suffer with her. I can't kill the woman Lucy loved.

So I can't let my anger overwhelm me like Palmer is doing. I have to stay strong. I have to let Palmer break down. Only then will her pain overtake her anger. Only then will I be able to convince her to let me go.

Palmer's eyes drag down my body, taking in all the scars covering my skin like tattoos I never wanted.

"Obviously, you understand physical pain," she says.

I nod. "There is nothing you can do to me that can hurt me."

She bites her lip, and I see that she's not here. She's thinking about something else, not about me.

I could let her be in her own head. It would prolong the pain from happening. But I need her to break, and I need her to break now. Every second I'm here is another second Julian or Bishop could be hurting Siren. I can't waste one second.

"Palmer? You were saying? Or are you so distracted by my hot body that you can't even imagine hurting me?"

She hisses, her viciousness coming back. "I can see why Lucy loved you. You and I are more alike than we are different. Luckily, that means I know how to hurt you. I know your weaknesses because they are the same as mine."

I look into her muddy brown eyes. I flick past the anger, trying to find the pain, but it's buried so deep within her that I'm not sure I can bring it up to the surface. I have to try —for Siren and Lucy.

"Then do it. Hurt me. Take vengeance on my flesh. Do it for Lucy," I growl.

Palmer snaps. She slaps me across the cheek, her anger pushing her to do something she's probably never done before.

I hear the slap, but I don't feel it. I'm sure it was vicious. I'm sure she used all of her force trying to hurt me. I'm sure my face is red from her handprint. But I don't feel it. I rarely feel physical pain, and right now, I'm so focused on Siren that Palmer could shoot me and throw me into a fire, and I wouldn't feel it. All I want is to go find Siren.

"Don't talk about Lucy," she says.

"Why? She was mine before she was yours. I can talk about Lucy all I want."

Slap.

SLAP.

I huff, my chest rising and falling hard at the double hit. I feel the familiar surge of my own anger taking hold. I'm not used to letting people hurt me without trying to fight back. But I won't fight back. Even if I get free of my chains, I won't hurt Palmer, for Lucy.

"Lucy loved me," she says.

"And before *you*, she loved *me*," I say calmly back. It's true, but I only say it to feed her anger. The only way she'll let her pain in is when her anger is at its height. When all of her walls are down, and her rage is on full display, that's my chance to break her.

This time, it's a punch. My head snaps again to the side, as her force hits my jaw. It's a good punch, but it will hurt her hand more than my jaw.

"Fuck," she curses, shaking her hand.

I raise a brow, staring at her. "Is that all you got? All you are going to do to the man who took the love of your life from you? The man who loved her before you and then discarded her like she was nothing." *Lucy, forgive me. I always loved you, but I'm going to say whatever it takes to get back to Siren.*

Palmer frowns, stepping back like she's considering my words. There is no snarky comeback, and that scares me. My comments are meant to rile her up, to let her inner beast out, not to make her introspective.

She pulls out her phone.

"What are you doing? Can't hurt me on your own?" I ask.

I'm right. I realize it as soon as she speaks on the phone. She's calling down her reinforcements.

Fuck.

I curse, not because I'm afraid of what the men upstairs can do to me. They can physically hurt me more than Palmer can, especially in an unfair fight where I'm chained up. But I need Palmer to be the one to hurt me. I need her to be the one who touches me, to make it personal. That way, she unleashes her anger. If she stands back and watches other people hurt me, I'll never break her.

I hear the men from upstairs file down the stairs.

Palmer grins, thinking she's won.

"Really? This is what you want? To watch someone else do your dirty work? I thought you were stronger than that. I thought we were the same. I thought you took care of your own business," I say.

She leans forward until her breath is on my ear.

"Scared, Zeke? I thought you weren't afraid of anything. Physical pain doesn't scare you. These men can hurt you more than I ever could, so you should be afraid."

She steps back, but she's still less than a foot away from me. I could head-butt her, knee her, hurt her if I wanted to, but I don't. I have to protect her while going after Siren.

My eyes glance behind her at the three men who now occupy the basement with us. One has biceps that make him look like a professional baseball player. I'm sure he can punch like he's hitting a home run. Another is slim and lanky; I don't have to worry about him being able to rip flesh from my bones.

But the third man is a monster. His biceps bulge, his shoulders are built, his thighs thick—he's as big as me. I know what I'm capable of. Even if he isn't as talented as me, it just takes muscles and a little bit of darkness in your heart to be able to do damage to another human being's body. I check his eyes; he has the darkness.

He may not be as skilled as I am at torture, but he doesn't have to be to leave more scars on my body.

I cut back to Palmer, "I'm not afraid of being physically hurt. Your men can torture me all day; I know how to withstand it. But if you prevent me from saving the woman I love, you will regret it. When the anger is gone and replaced with the pain, you'll realize the woman I love was there when the woman you love died. I know in my heart she did everything she could to protect and save her. You'll regret letting her suffer when you come to your senses, when you realize torturing me won't bring her back. You'll regret this."

She grinds her teeth and breathes out her anger through her nostrils. Her eyes flicker side to side.

Did I get through to her?

"I won't regret this," she says, and steps back. All the way back, out of reach. Her eyes never leave mine.

I'm the one who breaks eye-contact when I close my eyes, going to my hardened space that will protect me until the physical pain is over. Palmer may think she's tough, but she's never seen torture. She's never seen what is about to happen to me. Maybe that's enough to break her.

My mind flickers to Siren, thinking I should stay with her to help me get through the pain. My love for her will get me through.

I feel the first punch to my stomach. My body reacts. My abs tighten, my body falls back, but I can't slump all the way back as the chains grip my wrists and ankles, keeping me in place. But the part I hate the most is the sound I make—a wretched sound as my lungs burn trying to get air, and my stomach clenches, trying to keep from vomiting from the force.

I hate that I made a sound.

I hate that I showed that I can feel physical pain.

I can't associate this painful moment with Siren, so I can't let her save me.

Kai is my next thought. The last time I was tortured, she saved me. But I won't let me save her either.

Lucy?

No.

I won't let any woman save me. I won't let any man save me either. I've withstood torture before. This is no different. I just have to go to my dark place, and hope that when this is over, I can escape the darkest depths of my heart and return to Siren.

5

SIREN

I SURRENDER.

I never thought I'd say those words, but Julian did. From the moment I started working for him, he knew. He knew that eventually, I'd be his.

I take a deep breath, gathering courage from all the oxygen in the room. Taking on the strength of any ghosts, spirits, and souls. Gaining power from all the gods and divine beings. Pulling from all the crystals, celestial beings, and deities. Calling on all the martyrs and saints. I need the strength of all of them to survive this, whether I believe in their existence or not. And even then, it won't be enough.

The only person who could help me is the one person who is isn't here—Zeke.

"One step at a time, my little Aria. I wish you just saying the words would be enough and we could fuck like lovers, but you aren't ready yet."

My eyes cut through him.

"Kiss me like you want me. That's the first step to falling in love with me," Julian says.

There it is. He wants me to love him. *Not a chance in hell.*

I step forward. He stays still, waiting for me this time.

I can't do this.

I can't kiss him.

I can't fuck him.

I don't even think I could lie there and let him fuck me, but what he's asking for is so much more than just letting him violate me. He's asking me to give him myself.

I inch closer, except my inches are more like millimeters. At this rate, it's going to take me all year to get close enough to kiss him. *Fine by me.*

"Siren," Julian says.

I freeze. He never calls me Siren. I'm always Aria, never Siren.

"Siren," Julian says again, and I realize what he is doing. He's trying to make it easier for me.

I lean forward, as he says the name that Zeke calls me. I can feel the heat of his breath, but I can't move the final inch.

"I can't," I breathe. *I can't fuck him like he's Zeke. I can't grab him and kiss him. I just can't...*

Julian nods. "I always knew you had a weakness. I just didn't realize it would be a man."

He walks behind me, setting the glass down on the bedside table behind me. I still don't stare at the bed. I can't. I won't. There is no bed. Nothing is going to happen.

"What are you going to do? What do you want?" I breathe out, my voice quieter than ever. I'm usually strong and determined. In a normal situation, I can fight back. But fighting back this time means death to the one person I love above all else. I know in my heart that if I fight, Julian will go after the person I love. He will go after my "weakness." He'll go after Zeke.

Julian doesn't look at me. "I thought you were a romantic candles and flowers type of girl, Siren."

There is a crack of lighting overhead. I jump at the sound and turn my head in the direction. And then I see it—*the bed.*

It's the most exquisite, romantic bed I've ever seen. I didn't think beds could be romantic, but this one is. This one is clouds of white pillows covered in gold trim. Pink and red rose petals are scattered all over it. The candles illuminate it and the stars sparkle down on top of it, making the bed is every woman's dream. This bed would make two people feel like the only two people in the world.

I turn my head, trying to understand how the evil monster behind me could ever want to make love to a woman in a bed like this. I search, but I no longer see Julian out of the corner of my eye.

Fuck.

I turn quickly, but it's too late.

The door opens, and as I expected, four men run in, each grabbing one of my limbs before I can fight back. I'm tied to the beautiful bed that should be my heaven. Instead, it will be my hell.

The men retreat as quickly as they came, and I'm left alone with Julian.

"We will start slowly, with something easy to surrender to. I thought I'd never have you until you gave yourself to me completely, but I realize now, it will take time for you to want me. Which is why I won't discuss all the vows and promises you have made to me, yet. Right now, we will focus on the first step..." his voice trails off. Maybe my brain is shutting down in preparation for what is about to happen.

I begin praying to every god I don't believe in.

None of them come, none of them save me.

Zeke...

I need you. Please, save me.

I stare at the door in the corner, begging it to open. For Zeke to be on the other side. He'd be here if he could, but something is stopping him. Something is keeping him away.

I feel a needle stab into my arm. My mind ignites into a blur of images.

"This will help make you mine," Julian says. At least I think it's Julian.

Fuck, my head is spinning. I can't focus. Between the drugs and being tied up, I won't be able to fight. I won't be able to stop it. I won't be able to tell Zeke I did everything to keep him off of me, to prevent this from happening.

I'm right there, Siren. I'm right there.

I close my eyes, and I hear Zeke's voice so clearly. I feel him everywhere. My anchor keeping me out of the darkness Julian is trying to pull me into.

Don't fight me; you know you love me. You know you want me. Let me make you feel so good.

Suddenly I know how Zeke is going to save me. He's going to ensure Julian isn't the one who fucks me. He's going to take over my dreams, my thoughts, my desires—all I see now is Zeke.

"You want it rough, Siren?"

I shiver at the thought of my big bad man taking me roughly. I love having Zeke both ways. Slow and tender, and rough and fast. I can feel the walls of my pussy tightening at the thought of Zeke entering me fast. Of him pushing me to my limits. Of his teeth sinking into my flesh. His fingers fisting my hair, pulling it hard, bringing all the blood to each part of my body he marks.

"Yes," I hiss. I want it rough. It's been too long since I had Zeke. I need him now. I can't wait.

"Good girl," he says.

"No, I'm a bad girl. Very bad. I need to be punished."

Zeke chuckles, loving who I am. I'm not a good girl. I'm his bad girl. I'm the woman who would kill for him, not caring whose life I had to take to ensure he survives. That's who I am.

"Oh, don't worry, Siren, I'll punish you." His voice sounds darker than it usually is—not just growly, or husky, but heavier than I've ever heard it before.

It startles me, and the haze begins to lift. I remember what I'm pushing down, what my subconscious is protecting me from.

I'm there. It's me, not him, Zeke's voice says again.

I feel the bed dip, and then his hips sink down on top of mine. "God, I've wanted you for so long. How much do you want me?" he says, his hips pressing harder over mine.

I roll my hips up, trying to get him to stop teasing me and give me what I want. He lifts up, preventing me from feeling his cock until I answer him.

"More than I want to breathe, that's how badly I want you, Zeke." He grunts, but still doesn't give me any physical connection except for where his thighs press against my hips.

I feel his hand against my face, stroking my cheek. I close my eyes, leaning against the softness of his hand.

I frown, usually Zeke's hands are rough, cut up, and calloused.

Shh, it's me, Siren. You know it's me, Zeke.

So I keep my eyes closed, my toes tingling as his big strong hands stroke down my cheek to my neck. His face dips to my neck as he presses his lips beneath my ear. So smooth, he shaved for me.

I squirm as the light kisses tingle down my body.

"Zeke," I moan again. I need more. I need him to punish me. I need him to fuck me.

Something deep in my mind says I need this over.

Why would I want this over? All I want is Zeke. Over and over and over.

I arch my back, my wrists and ankles pulling gently on the metal handcuffs, keeping me from touching Zeke.

"What do you want?" he asks.

"For you to touch me, punish me, fuck me."

I feel the blade then, and I smile—finally.

The blade slips under the neck of my shirt, and he pulls down, shredding my shirt.

"Aww," I moan as I feel the blade of the knife trailing down the center of my chest, over my breast bone, digging in just enough to inject into my skin and cause a line down the center of my body that will remind me of this night forever.

Good, I want to remember.

No, you don't.

I push the words in my head out, so confused by all the voices in my head.

"More," I say without him asking.

The knife slides into my soaked pants, soaked from both the rain and my excitement. The knife struggles against the thickness of the material and, at one point, jabs into my thigh.

"Fuck," I cry at the pain, my eyes starting to jolt open. Quickly his lips are on me, and I fall back down, my body relaxing a little as his lips push against mine. His tongue inserts into my mouth, begging for forgiveness for hurting me.

I forgive you, my tongue says back. My mouth opens wider, inviting more of him in. I can't get enough of Zeke. His mouth takes away my pain, but then I shiver. I'm still soaked from the rain, and although the kisses are nice, they aren't enough to heat my body.

"You're so scared," he says.

"What?" I say, my voice catching, my confusion and embarrassment at being scared instead of flawlessly beautiful for Zeke.

"Don't. Don't try to hide. I love the scars. I love how much pain you can endure."

I bite my lip. "Punish me." I want to feel more pain.

"I'm going to cover every one of your scars with a mark of my own, so when you look at them, you think of me," he says.

"Perfect," I say back, loving the idea of it.

"This mark over your neck is now mine," he says.

I feel the sharp point of the knife. I jolt at the pain, my eyes watering, my stomach heaving trying to get him to stop.

"Fuck, Zeke," I say at the pain.

He kisses me, and I forget the pain.

"This breast is mine," he says, and I feel the scrape over the upper curve of my breast, where a bullet grazed me.

I bite my lip to keep my scream in. I want him to cover my scars with his own, but fuck does this hurt.

"Tell me you want me to mark you."

"I want you to mark me."

"Tell me you want me to fuck you."

"Fuck me, Zeke."

He growls like I said something wrong, but I can't think what it would be.

"Tell me you want me to fuck you," he tries again.

Maybe he didn't hear me the first time?

"I want you to fuck me, Zeke."

He growls, and then I feel his thick cock pushing at my entrance.

Something's wrong.

I got you, it's me. I'm going to fuck you. Think of me.

Zeke, my anchor, my love.

I don't have to open my eyes to know it's him as he pushes inside me in one hard stroke. My body stretches, letting him in, adjusting to him. I wait for him to thicken, for him to consume all of my body, but it never comes.

This isn't Z—

I love you, stay with me.

And then he's thrusting. He's pushing over and over. Drilling inside me with so much force that I hear the bed cracking. That's my Zeke. That's my dangerous strong man who loves me so much that he breaks the bed.

I pull against the handcuffs, trying to grab onto Zeke, to feel his hair, his muscles, but I can't break free.

"Zeke, I want to feel you," I say.

"Shut up, bitch."

"What?" I snap, not believing he said that. I must have heard wrong.

His lips hover over mine again. "I want to hear you scream."

"Zeke," I howl as he hits me deep.

"No, not my name, just scream," he says, and then he's digging his fingers into one of my fresh wounds.

I scream. I scream like I've never screamed before. I like

when Zeke punishes me, when he pushes my limits, but this is different. This isn't punishment; this is sin.

"Zeke," I moan, trying to get him to stop. Suddenly, I feel the knife against my nipple. He slices, and I cry out again, the pain making me shake, and vomit rising in my throat.

"You like that, Siren?" he says.

No, I don't like it.

He thrusts again.

Hold onto me, listen to me. I got you. I'm not hurting you. I love you. I would never hurt you.

My eyes fly open, and I see *him.*

The man I've thought of as *he.*

He isn't Zeke.

He is Julian. And he's over me.

No, come back to me. Don't let him win. Let me protect you.

I close my eyes, taking a deep breath as I let my head and heart go back to Zeke. I let him protect me. I think of Zeke while Julian thrusts into me. As he cuts me with a knife, butchering my body like an animal.

I don't cry anymore. I don't moan. I give Julian nothing.

I give Zeke everything.

Zeke anchors me; he keeps me safe. My thoughts stay mine. My body remains mine. Everything is still mine.

I know that Julian pumped me full of drugs. I know that he tricked me into thinking he was Zeke so it would either ruin my images of Zeke or I would do what he wanted. Even with the handcuffs, Julian didn't believe that I wouldn't fight him. That he wouldn't feel in control of me.

Julian isn't in control of me. I'm not his; I'm Zeke's—always.

I feel Julian finishing inside me.

"Scream," he says, needing my pain to finish.

"No," I say, not giving Julian anything.

I feel the knife at my clit.

Fuck, no.

He wouldn't. Would he?

No, he wants me to be his. Julian wants me to give him my pleasure, and he won't be able to if he cuts off my clit.

I scream.

And Julian comes.

I finish in control by screaming the name that will drive Julian insane.

"Zeke!"

6

ZEKE

BLOOD DRIPS DOWN MY FOREHEAD, OOZING OVER MY BULGING eyes. It seeps into my nose until I'm breathing more blood than oxygen. I taste the rusty sting on my tongue.

My face is bloodied, bruised, and swollen. I can't feel. I can't see. I can't breathe. Blood mutes all of my senses.

I hang from my wrists, where metal cuffs encase them. I'm slumped forward, and the skin around my wrist is cut deep from my own weight. I'm sure the men have more than doubled the scars on my body. My shallow breaths indicate cracked and broken ribs.

From the way the room spins, it's clear I've lost a pint or more of blood.

My legs shake, barely holding me up, putting more weight on my wrists.

I stare down at my feet and see a mix of colors. Red, purple, blue mar my body. Bruises, gashes, welts.

I've gone to the dark place in my heart that knows I deserve this after I've done this to countless other men. To withstand torture, some men push everything out and go to a zen-like place. Others think of the one special person they love to help them get through it.

Some panic and scream, making a big fuss. Others grit and bear it.

I'm different than most. I feel every strike, punch, cut, slice, whip, kick. I feel it and let it become part of me. I let it feed my monster. It hardens me. It ensures I can do my job of protecting everyone. I've never lived for myself. I've never chosen me over someone else. I've never chosen love over ensuring my friends are safe.

The pain should be fueling me to fight back, to seek vengeance, and kill them all for what they've done to me. I should be plotting their deaths so they can never hurt any of my friends.

But I don't give a damn about protecting my friends in this moment. I don't care about protecting Enzo, or Langston, or Liesel, or even Kai. I don't think about honoring Lucy.

All I think about is saving Siren. I promised her. I love her. She's my everything. All I care about is Siren.

So while the pain is feeding the darkest part of my soul, it's also tunneling through toward Siren. Toward finding her, saving her, and loving her.

I can feel it in my bones. Someday I'm going to have to choose—her above everything else. That terrifies me. Not because I don't want to put her first, but because it will mean changing who I am at the most fundamental level. I'll no longer be the enforcer, the protector, the brute strength who is always saving everyone else.

I'll be the man in love. The man selfishly protecting his love.

I'll have to start over. Find a new job. Find a new identity. That transition scares me more than any of the four pairs of eyes staring back at me.

I don't see the people in front of me. The blood and haze of the shock to my body prevents me from actually seeing them, but I feel every single person.

All four people in this room took part in my torment and agony.

The three men took their swings at me, using their preferred methods to pull screams and cries out of me reflexively. Each used a different technique to mark my body.

As I guessed, the large man built most like me did the most damage and took the most pleasure in hurting me.

Palmer was quiet the whole time. She didn't speak. I didn't let myself look at her. I needed to stay strong and focused. I needed her to know I won't engage with her until it's just her and me again alone. The men will see through my plan and stop me. I need her alone.

Now that the beatings have stopped, I pull my head up. It takes all the muscles in my neck and back to lift my head the few inches up so I can glance at Palmer. My head has never felt heavier, and I'm only guessing where she is when I force my head up.

Now is the time. Now is the turning point.

I can't see what my body looks like, but I know I'm not a pretty sight. I'm sure I've never looked worse. If Palmer is going to let her own pain in, it will be now. It will be seeing me so physically damaged, but not giving a damn because there is a woman I love who I have to get to. I have to save Siren.

So I lift my thousand-pound head and find Palmer in the corner, smoking her damn cigarette like she's sitting on the sideline of a fair boxing match.

"Do you believe me now?" I croak out, trying to tell her I won't ever yield. I won't ever give up. She can destroy my body, rip me apart until I'm lying in pieces, but her anger will still be here. I won't let her feel like she's broken me, because I don't give a damn about my body. All I care about is getting Siren back.

Palmer has had her fun. Enough is enough.

I try to speak again, but all I end up doing is gargling blood.

"Should we kill him?" one of the men asks Palmer.

There is a momentary pause, and I think she's going to say yes. Maybe watching me deal with the pain hasn't been near as fun as she thought it would be, and she has no use for me anymore.

"No," she says, shocking the entire room.

I breathe calmly for the first time in hours. Not because I fear death, but I fear dying without ensuring Siren lives a long and happy life.

"Leave," Palmer says suddenly.

My eyes glaze, looking at her through the blood, wishing I could see what is going on in her head.

"But—" one of the men starts.

"Leave!" Palmer's voice shrieks through the room.

The three men stumble and run up the stairs, leaving Palmer and me alone—just like I want.

Now's my chance, *but how can I convince her when I can't even speak?*

My head falls, most likely looking like defeat from Palmer's perspective.

"You don't think you can be broken, do you?"

I moan, but can't speak as my head rolls side to side. I don't have the strength to lift it again.

Palmer walks to my ankles, and I hear the clink of the

key going into the lock. She removes the cuffs from my ankles, but I don't move. I'm barely standing on my feet, still putting most of my weight onto my wrists to hold me up.

She stands and undoes one of my wrists, letting me hang by one wrist. I know what's about to happen, and I can't stop it.

She walks to my other side and unlocks the other cuff holding me up.

I fall.

Hard onto the floor.

My body crumples into a broken ball on the floor.

Palmer takes her time. She stands over me, watching me, considering what she wants to do.

She gives me enough time to speak. "Do it for Lucy." Let me go for Lucy.

Her eyes gloss over, and I know I lost Palmer again. "Not until I break you."

She leans over me, grabbing one of the knives the men used, and she goes to work on my bloodied jeans. The knife scrapes into my legs as she rips my jeans from my body. It takes her a while, but eventually, she removes all the clothes from my body until I'm naked on the floor.

I can't fight her.

I can't stop her.

I can't even lift a finger.

She can do whatever she wants with me.

"Lucy loved you," she says.

I moan.

"I've been with men and women. I'm bisexual, just like Lucy. It's time to see what Lucy saw in you. It's time to take the one thing from you that might break you," Palmer says.

It's then I realize what's happening. She's going to use my body. Use me to cover up her pain. Try to force pain into me. Try to take away my control and make me feel like I'm hurting Siren by not stopping Palmer from using my body.

I open my eyes wide and look into Palmer's eyes. The lengths she will go to to prevent herself from feeling her own pain of losing Lucy are immense. Palmer has found my weakness. She knows how to break me.

And there is nothing I can do to stop her.

7

PALMER

"LUCY, IS THAT YOU?" I ASK, MY VOICE CATCHING IN MY throat at the sight of her. *She's here.*

Some-fucking-how, she's here.

"Yes," her sultry voice says. It's not angelic. It's not perfect. It's gritty and heart-wrenching. That's how I know this is real. She's not an angel. *This is fucking real.*

I feel the wetness in my eyes, sensing the waterfall about to start flowing down my face any second now. These are the last few moments I'm going to have clear vision.

"I thought you were dead," I say, hiccuping on the last word from a lack of oxygen. This is it—the last moment I see Lucy clearly.

She's standing in front of me in dark jeans, a ripped red shirt, and Converse sneakers. Her hair is parted to the extreme on one side, and her lips are painted red.

Lucy looks fierce, like she came here to demand I go into battle with her. I will. I'll do anything for her. I'm just so relieved that she's here. *But is she still mine?*

Lucy runs to me, and our arms fling around each other in a death grip. The fountain of tears streaming down my face doesn't let me see her, but I can still feel her. The curve of her ass against my hand, her soft breasts pushed against mine, our foreheads pressed together.

"Kiss me," I say, not able to even see her bright lips through my tears and joy at her being alive.

Her hands grab my cheeks, and then we are kissing, suffocating, and exhaling. Neither of us can breathe through the kisses, tears, and general lack of oxygen. We can live off each other's kisses, though, forever. Neither of us stop. Neither of us step back to let the other come up for air. We need each other more than we need to live.

I push Lucy back, and she falls to a heap on the floor.

We both laugh at how uncoordinated she is. I straddle her with my legs, pinning her to the floor. Lucy is small, about half my size. I love that I can dominate her. She may be the fierce one, the leader of our two-person team in public, but in the bedroom, I rule.

Lucy's lazy, sexy eyes seem to agree with me.

I wipe my tears on my shirt, hoping I'll stop crying now that she's here and she's still mine.

"You smell like smoke," Lucy says with a frown as she grabs the neck of my shirt and yanks me toward her.

I kiss her again. "Do you care?"

"Yes, because I want you around for a long fucking time."

"Why?"

"Because you are mine."

"Are you sure? Are you sure your heart doesn't still belong to Zeke?" I feel the ache in my chest. This is what I was most afraid of, getting her back only to realize she's still in love with him, not me.

"I love you, Palmer. I used to love Zeke, but that was

before I met you. He was my darkness; you are my light. You are the reason I'm alive. You are the reason I live."

"Dammit, stop making me cry. I want to see you when I fuck you," I say through more fucking tears.

Lucy laughs and then palms my breast beneath my shirt. I arch my back at the warm feelings zipping through my body at her touch. "Feel me first; you can look at me the second time. Just feel me."

I moan as she palms my other breast in her small, delicate hands. This time her thumb brushes over my hardened nipple. I'm gone—my eyes are never opening again. I just want to feel everything.

"Fuck me, Palmer. Take control. Punish me like you're pissed I left you. Fuck me like you won't ever let me leave again."

She doesn't have to ask me twice.

I growl, then I grab her shirt and rip it off over her head as my mouth comes down on her smooth stomach. I start off soft and light, knowing it will drive her wild and prep her for the harsh, teeth bearing kisses I'm about to give her body.

Lucy doesn't move beneath me, probably from the shock of seeing me again. It doesn't matter if she moves, just that she's here. I can do all the work.

My mouth moves its way up her body, tasting every inch, each kiss becoming rougher than the previous. I nip at her nipples, sink my claws into her neck, and kiss her ears. I love every second that I get to worship her skin again.

Lucy moans when I yank on her hair. It's low and deep and unlike her normal sounds. It just drives me to work harder, because I love the guttural sounds she's making.

"I love it when you growl like that for me. I'm going to

make you scream like you've never screamed before," I whisper into her ear before biting down hard on her lobe.

She squeals.

I come alive again for the first time in months.

I grab the hem of my shirt and yank it off. I grab her hands and place them on my bare breasts. Her hands somehow seem bigger than they were a minute before, but I ignore the weirdness.

"Rub me," I command.

She doesn't move.

That's how it's going to be. She wants to defy me, so I'll punish her. I grin. I'm going to enjoy this.

I put my hands on top of hers and rub her fingers over my nipples as my hips continue to pin down her narrow hips. I rub myself over her body, but I want more. So much more.

I feel my core heating, my clit tingling in my pants, wanting to feel my skin against hers.

I lean down, my long hair framing her face as I kiss her tenderly. She doesn't kiss me back. So I suck on my lip, pulling another groan out of her.

I grin.

"I want you. All of you."

"Take me."

I scoot back on her body, my hands roaming, and I am delighted to find she's already naked for me. I drag my nails over her bare skin.

She hisses like it hurts, but I don't understand why. I'm not touching her hard enough to leave a mark.

I laugh. "Always the dramatic one." I kiss her inner thigh, and she stops.

I smirk as I begin to undress. I know the way to my woman's heart. I know her body better than anyone, even

Zeke. I've loved her longest. Tonight, I'm going to remind her that she doesn't get to leave me just because things get tough. She's mine. For as long as both our hearts are beating.

I struggle to get my pants down over my thighs, but I finally succeed, falling back on my ass on her feet.

We both laugh at how ridiculous it is, but it doesn't change the intensity of the mood. I want her—desperately and wholly. I want to hear her scream my name. Nothing is going to stop that from happening.

I finish shoving my own pants and underwear down, and then I go back to straddling her hips, my hands cupping her head tenderly. As much as I want it rough, as I want to punish her, I can't—not now. I love her too much.

Right now, I just want to celebrate this beautiful moment. Of finding her again. Of her being in my life again. Of being reunited.

"I love you, Lucy, so fucking much," I say, tears falling down my cheeks like lava down a volcano. It burns because I can't see her, filling my eyes and falling slowly. It's not a river that pours out of me, leaving me with only good feelings. These tears hurt.

"I love you, too."

"Make love to me," I say.

"Every chance I get," she says back.

I grin, loving our little saying. It's always the same.

I push Lucy's legs apart and slip my hands between her legs, but what I find surprises me.

"Oh, is that how you want it? You want to fuck me with a strap-on?"

"Mmmm," she moans.

I bite my lip, considering telling Lucy I don't want any

toys or devices. I don't want a vibrator or a dildo or any rubber between us. I just want her.

But I can't tell her that. She's obviously thought through how she wants to have me the first time back to already have it strapped on.

"Okay, I'll fuck you however you want me to." I kiss her forehead. I start rubbing myself in slow, methodical circles as I straddle her waist. My eyes are still closed, and the tears are still falling, but I don't need to see Lucy to feel her. She's all around me. She wants to be inside me.

"Please, hurry," I hear her pant. If I wasn't wet before, I am now. I'm soaked, and I rub my wetness all over her belly.

"I'm so fucking wet for you. No one gets me this wet, only you."

And then I grab the plastic cock, and I ride her. I feel myself stretch as the cock fits inside me, I make sure to sink all the way down until our clits are rubbing over each other, and then I begin to rock.

"You like that?"

More moans. She's speechless, that's how much she likes it.

I massage her breasts as I rock over her. It feels so fucking good. Somehow, the rubber cock seems to get harder the longer I pump over it.

Hmm, it must be one of those high-tech cocks meant to resemble the real thing?

I really don't care about how real the strap-on resembles a cock. I just care about Lucy.

I lean forward as I continue to ride her, and then I kiss her again as my hand tangles in her hair. I pull roughly when she doesn't open up for me.

"Going to make me work for it, huh, Lucy?"

I push my way inside her mouth and find her delicious

tongue. I massage it, and finally, she gives in, circling my tongue with hers. I feel the moisture building in my walls, fucking the cock. I want it out, though, because I just want her.

"I want you, Lucy. I just want you."

"Then have me. Any way you want me, I'm yours."

I grin. "Thank god."

I go to climb off her and rip the fake cock off her. But I feel her trembling, and I know what that means. She's about to come without me. I don't give a damn that it's our first time together in months and we aren't coming together. I just want her to enjoy this moment. I want her to come as many times as she can.

"Come for me, baby. Come."

I rock harder, knowing the friction on her pussy is what is getting her off. So I ride the cock in longer, faster strokes.

"Come for me, Lucy," I scream, and somehow the thought of her coming brings me right there too. And then we are both coming. I'm screaming, she's screaming. It's the most beautiful, painful sound.

It sounds like coming home, but it also feels fleeting. *How many more times are we going to get to do this?* She came back, but she still has cancer. She's still dying. She still refuses to save herself for me.

I'm about to open my mouth and ask if she is ready to be selfish, do the right thing to save herself, when I feel her coming.

Lucy isn't a squirter. She never comes like this.

Suddenly, everything hits me like a truck ramming into my head.

The tears stop.

The screaming stops.

The fear and anger return, along with a new emotion I've been trying to hold back.

An emotion I dare not name for fear it will become more powerful.

I squeeze my eyes shut, my brain already processing what's happening. It's already telling me I'm about to lose everything I love all over again.

Reality and my imagination mixed in such a fucked up way to try and give me a few more moments of peace, but there is no peace for a woman like me. There is no happiness for a woman who lost the light that guided her way— the beauty in a room of darkness. There is no rest for the wicked, and I am definitely wicked. I'm going to hell for the sins I've committed tonight.

"Shh, it's okay. You are going to be okay," her voice morphs into his, and I realize I'm sobbing again, my shoulders shaking as I still sit on his now soft cock.

What did I do?

And why did I think it would make me feel better to take a man who Lucy once loved?

Why did I think hurting another would heal me? All it did was open a deeper wound.

"Take it one step at a time," his voice says again.

And why is HE comforting me? I had Zeke tortured by three men. And then when he was so broken that he couldn't fight back, I raped him like he was Lucy.

He should hate me. He should want to kill me.

I rest my hand on his chest and feel the unstable beat of his heart. He's conflicted and in pain. The breaths he takes are shallow. If he takes a deep breath, the agony will rip through his entire chest, diaphragm, and gut. He keeps them light and shallow to avoid further injury, but because of his shallow breathing, he never gets a big, healing breath. Never enough to calm himself.

"Fuck!" I scream, my nails digging into his chest.

I pound my hand over his chest in a fist. Pissed at him for not fighting me off. Pissed at myself for turning into a demon. And pissed at the world for taking Lucy.

It should have been me. I should have been the one to die.

Yes, that's it!

I form a plan in my head. A way to end the pain I'm in. This—this heartache, this stabbing, throbbing, loss—I know that no matter how long I live, it will never leave me. Never, never, never.

Lucy was the only person who understood me.

She understood that I hate chocolate but love M&Ms.

She understood that I love the ocean, but hate the sand.

She understood that I loved her, while also loving men.

She understood that I am a complex, misunderstood, broken woman who shouldn't have been able to heal from the wounds society inflicted at being different, but I did because she walked the road with me.

She was my shield when someone would yell profanities at us, tell us we went against nature, tell us we were going to hell for being ourselves. None of it mattered because of Lucy. She made all of it bearable. Not easy, but she made every profanity worth it.

And now, she's gone.

She's not coming back.

She's just gone.

And I wasn't there when she needed me the most. I wasn't fucking there. She failed me by pushing me away. By not fighting and taking the drugs she needed to survive, screwing everyone else. And I failed her by not finding a way to be with her when she took her last breath.

We both failed.

We both lost.

The only way I can remedy that is to join Lucy in hell. There is no fucking way two badass women like us are going to heaven.

I smile. A genuine full smile. I'm only moments away from ending the pain, from finding peace, from being reunited with Lucy.

Yes, I know what I have to do. I have to end this...

8

ZEKE

Palmer's demeanor changes from unbearable pain to impenetrable peace in the span of a few seconds. I know what it means—she's found a way to end her pain.

She's planning on killing herself.

I can see it on her face. For a moment, I see it as the right path for her too. She's so fucking happy thinking about joining Lucy that it's hard not to let her die to be with her.

But it's not what Lucy would want, and despite the pain this woman has inflicted on my body, and the amount of heartbreak she has brought me at not saving Siren sooner, I can't condemn her to death either.

Palmer is just in pain. A pain I hope to never understand.

Please, let Siren still be alive. Let her be whole. Let her still love me.

Palmer is still on top of me, my dick is still inside her, and I've never been so disgusted at a woman, at myself. *I fucking came in her! What is wrong with me?* I should have been able to control myself.

I didn't want her, but my body took over. I had no control once she started thrusting over me. The only way to stop myself from coming would have been to push her off me.

I didn't have the physical strength, though. I still don't. That's why until she decides to move, my cock will continue to rest inside her, in a place it doesn't belong.

I feel sick. I want to vomit.

Forgive me, Siren. Please, forgive me.

I close my eyes, keeping the tears in. It's the only part of my body I can currently control.

I can't control my breathing. My broken ribs poking into my lungs only allow me to take short, shallow breaths.

I can't control my heartbeat. It's erratic and racing, scared those men are going to come back into the room and beat me again.

I can't control my muscles. I try. My brain fires, begging my muscles to move. But there is either a break in the connection, or more likely, my muscles just say fuck off because they have taken such a rough beating.

And my fucking cock—don't get me started on that bastard. He's betrayed me more than any other part of me. He had no problem getting hard when a naked woman climbed on top of me and kissed me. He thought it was perfectly fine to enjoy the ride when she sank down over him and milked me dry. He came like it was his right. I want to chop him off for betraying Siren like that.

I swallow hard, trying to push all those thoughts down. There is nothing I can do but go to Siren and ask for the forgiveness I don't deserve but desperately need.

Palmer continues to sit happily on top of me. She bends over, reaching for something I can't make out because I don't have the strength to even turn my fucking head to see.

I'm disappointed when she rights herself on me again, and I see the glint of metal reflecting the light from overhead into my eyes.

"Palmer, don't," I croak out, coughing up more blood.

She sees me, really sees me, since the first time she started fucking me. For the past thirty minutes, she's been in some sort of hypnotic state. She's been seeing me as Lucy, and nothing I said broke her spell.

"I have to," she says, gripping the knife still in front of her. For a second, I think this is going to turn into a murder-suicide, but I don't think she's angry at me anymore. The anger has been displaced by her pain. That's her only focus.

"No, you don't. I know it hurts now, but it won't always be this way."

She whimpers. "Yes, it will. It will always hurt. I'll always feel like I'm drowning, the water will be crashing down on me, but I'll never die. Nor will I ever be able to come up for enough oxygen to sustain me. All I've ever feel is the pain of drowning without it ever ending. I need it to end."

"It will. Trust me. One day, you'll wake up, and the pain will just be gone. It won't be suffocating and trying to kill you anymore. You just have to get through this."

"I can't."

"You can. Let me help you."

"I can't live like this for one hour, let alone the years it will take to get rid of this pain."

"It won't take years."

"How long then?"

I bite my lip. I could lie to her and say only a couple days, but that's not true. I don't know how long it will take.

"More than days, less than years," I say.

"Weeks?"

"Maybe, maybe more, maybe less."

"I can't." She breaks. She can't hold on another second. She slashes her left wrist in one quick sweep. Even if I could move my muscles properly, I wouldn't have been able to stop her, she was so quick.

I stare at her wrist as a small cord of blood drips down her forearm. She gasps in relief, like she can finally breathe for the first time in years. The pain from her wrist takes over from the pain of losing Lucy.

The wound she created is mostly superficial. Sure, if left unattended long enough, she would die from blood loss, maybe. But I'm here. Her guards are here. Right now, all she needs is a bandage, maybe a couple of stitches, and she would survive easily.

I can still save her—for Lucy.

What about Siren?

I can't save Siren until Palmer is dealt with. I'll have a better chance of asking for Siren's forgiveness if I save Palmer and don't let my own anger take hold of me.

"Palmer, give me the knife," I say in the commanding voice I use when I mean business. I don't let the blood clogging my throat prevent me from speaking in my affirmative, dominating way.

Her eyes open, and she stares at me, her hand lifting toward me. She's going to do it. She's in such a state that she just needs me to command her. She needs a leader to follow.

But she stops just short and quickly slices at her arm again, her face lighting up like she just won the lottery instead of having a knife cut into her flesh.

I wince at how deep the second cut is. She could bleed out in an hour from this cut. Not could, will.

I try to move my useless arm next to my body.

MOVE!

My fingers twitch. It's good to know I can feel my fingers, and no nerve damage was done, but that's not reassuring when I have a grief-stricken woman holding a knife that I need to stop. However, knowing that I can move my arm again someday and being able to now, is very different.

I try my legs. One swift kick would knock her off me and hopefully remove the knife from her hand.

Stabbing pain shoots up my spine when I try to move my leg. *Come on, fight through it.*

I get my thigh an inch off the ground before it snaps back.

"Argh!" I scream out in pain.

Palmer watches me yelling, and I can't tell what's going through her mind.

Pain? Sorrow? Heartbreak? What does she feel when she sees me in torment?

"Shh, it's okay," she strokes my cheek. "Once I'm gone, you can call for help. Your body will heal. And then you can find your woman."

This is my chance. "I need to go now, Palmer. Siren is in trouble. Bad men have her—the same men who let Lucy die. I need you to help me. Call your guards down here and tell them we need an ambulance for us both. We need to heal, then together, we can go save Siren."

She stares at me like I just sprouted a second head.

"Palmer, you would like my Siren. Lucy even liked her, and you and I both know Lucy doesn't like many people." I chuckle, trying to lighten the mood. "But Lucy liked Siren. Help me get her back."

"I can't. I'm sorry."

NO!

This is it—the moment Palmer does something she can't take back.

I have to stop her, or I'll never get the forgiveness I need. From myself. From Lucy. From Siren.

I can't move my limbs, but I realize I can move my core. Palmer moves the knife to her throat. I'm afraid my movements will push the knife into her body instead of knocking it out of her hand, but it's my only chance.

I roll us, my body flipping on my side, my cock finally slipping out of her, and then gravity takes over. My heavy, lifeless body slumps on top of hers.

I watch as her hands drop to my chest, trying to keep me from crushing her or taking the knife from her.

The knife is no longer near her throat.

I did it!

But then...*FUCK!* A sound comes out of me I've never produced. I've been tortured, even been tortured in my sensitive area, but the way the knife slices into my balls is like nothing I've ever experienced before.

I saved Palmer, but as I cry through the pain moments before I blackout, I realize I just ended the Kane line. There will be no little Kanes. No baby Zekes or baby Sirens running around. I thought I was okay with that. I shouldn't have been selfish and wanted to bring kids into our world anyway.

But the moment the knife slices into my testicles, I mourn the loss of something I wanted desperately. Not only do I have to ask Siren for forgiveness for sleeping with another woman, but I have to ask for forgiveness for saving another woman while taking something so precious from both Siren and myself.

We will never have kids. This sealed it. And it's fucking painful. So goddamn painful I'll never be able to catch my breath again.

9

SIREN

I LIE IN A CLOUD OF PILLOWS, COMFORTERS, AND BLANKETS IN the center of the most beautiful room I've ever been in. My memories are scattered in my head. Unlike any other time I've been drugged, I want to keep my memories jostled. I don't want to put the pieces back together. My foggy memory is the only thing saving me.

My hand rests on my naked belly stroking up and down to calm the hunger pains. But it doesn't stop my stomach from growling, trying to convince me to go get food.

I can't do anything about my hunger. I'm trapped in this room. No matter how beautiful it is, it's still a cage. I'm still the wild animal that has to be locked inside.

But I don't feel wild anymore. My fight is gone. I don't do anything about the scratches, blood, and sweat covering my naked body. I don't try to cover up with blankets. I don't try to do something about the pain between my legs.

I just lie on the bed face up, bare for the world.

No, for Zeke.

This was Zeke's work. This is all a game. Zeke is in control. He knows what my body needs. I'm not eating because he wants my senses heightened when he fucks me. This isn't blood—this is lube and cum. My body isn't in pain —it's just sore from his touch.

My brain keeps my focus on Zeke instead of the truth. I used to only be able to speak the truth; now, all I can tell is a lie. I can't think of the truth. The truth will kill me. So I'll keep lying to myself. I'll keep hiding from the sin that was created here in this room, and I'll hope that someday, Zeke can pull the truth out of me again, and we will be strong enough to survive it.

I try to take a deep, calming breath, but my breath is shaky and light. Inhaling fully requires me to feel my entire body, something I just can't do.

Instead, I focus on my stomach. It groans. I can focus on hunger. Hunger is safe. Hunger won't lead me to thinking about anything dangerous.

I hear the door open.

No, no, no, no...I'm not ready. I can't handle more.

Zeke and I have fucked twenty-three times. I don't know how many days have passed, but I've counted three moons. Maybe it's been longer than that and I was just asleep, but not many. My body is tired and sore and weak. I can't handle more sex.

"No," I moan, unable to lift my eyelids. I'm so tired. Just let me sleep. I'll be ready for you in the morning after a good night of sleep, Zeke.

But of course, Zeke doesn't leave me alone. His appetite is insatiable. Sex is never enough. He wants me all day, every day.

I feel him standing over the bed, staring down at me with his intense eyes and heavy breath. Even though he's three feet away, I can still feel his warm breath like a fire roasting my body, hoping I'll come alive for him.

My body can't...he broke me. My body is incapable of being turned on anymore. I don't get excited from his kisses, his touch, his gaze.

I used to get excited when Zeke walked into the room, but now, I don't even get turned on when he's inside me. We have to use lube because I'm not wet enough. Even a vibrator doesn't get me off.

Sex no longer feels good to me because of Zeke. The man I love ruined sex for me.

No, he couldn't have. There is something wrong with me.

"What are you doing?" the voice demands. It's not Zeke's, but I don't dare open my eyes. I know I've been hallucinating. I haven't had enough to eat or drink, and I keep seeing things, hearing people.

"Siren, open your eyes," he says.

"No, I can't. I can't fuck you, again. I can't..." I'm crying because I never thought I'd turn Zeke down, but I just can't. My body needs a break. Zeke and I like to play with my limits, but he's pushed me too far.

He chuckles. It's deep and unnerving, enough for me to want to open my heavy eyelids. I open them just a crack, and I realize the man in front of me isn't Zeke.

"No!" I cry, grabbing at the covers, trying to pull them over me and protect myself from this man, this monster.

Bishop grabs my wrist. "I'm not here to rape you."

I don't believe him. I kick, trying to get free. I throw a punch, landing on his neck. My aim is shit right now because I'm so exhausted and can't see. The room spins as I move, but I have to get free. I can't let Bishop touch me.

"Stop," Bishop commands, his voice booming.

"No! I won't let you rape me!" I scream. This time when I kick, my aim is perfect, and I hit him right in the balls.

He releases me, grabbing onto his crown jewels as he doubles over in pain.

I take the chance to run. I jump out of bed and run to the door, my brain becoming clearer and clearer. I grab the doorknob, but the door doesn't budge.

"Help!" I yell, slamming my fists on the door. Surely whoever is on the other side won't want me in here. He won't want to share. He won't let Bishop rape me.

I just don't let my brain name who 'He' is. It's too close to the truth. That truth will destroy me.

"Someone, please, help!" I yell some more, pounding my fists over and over, but the door is thick and soundproof. No one can hear. No one is coming to save me.

My arms are yanked back, and I'm shoved against the door, my face and stomach feeling the coolness of the thick door against my skin.

"Stop. No one is coming," Bishop says. He holds me at my wrists, but otherwise, he doesn't touch me. He doesn't press his front to my naked back. He doesn't drop his head to sniff my hair or caress my neck. He just stands behind me, holding me in place.

"How did you get in here?" I ask, knowing only one man has the ability to enter this room.

"You really want to ask that question? You think he's more powerful than me?"

"I think he's the man in charge and you follow his orders."

"Julian is merely a thug I use to get what I want; he's not in charge."

I wince when he says Julian's name, because it breaks a little of the illusion, but I quickly put my walls back up. It was Zeke. *Zeke, Zeke, Zeke...*

Bishop notices my change and doesn't continue to talk about Julian.

"I'm not going to rape you," he says, dropping his voice until it sounds almost like a lullaby.

"You're a man holding a naked woman hostage, in a soundproof room that only two men can enter. What's stopping you?" I ask, my heart thumping a million miles an hour.

"Did I rape you before?" he asks.

I think back to before, the last time this man held me captive. He didn't rape me. He didn't touch me in any sexual way, but he did fuck with my head.

"No, you didn't." I exhale, knowing I don't have to worry about him raping me. *Maybe he's gay? Maybe he doesn't find me attractive? Maybe he prefers to get his power in different ways?*

Bishop releases my hands and then takes a step back, preparing for me to attack him again.

I turn to face him, watching for his reaction to my nakedness. He doesn't glance down. Not once. His eyes stay on mine, like my eyes alone hold all of my secrets.

"Are you gay?" I ask, needing to know why he won't look at me.

He smirks. "No."

That's it—one word. That's all I get. I know nothing about this man other than he's fit, tall, and handsome in a pretty-boy sort of way. He's muscular, but not as big as Zeke.

He has scars similar to mine on his arms, but that doesn't seem to be where his pain comes from. It comes from a woman. The love of his life that desperately hurt him.

"Who hurt you?" I ask, trying to understand this man.

"You already know."

I frown, racking my brain for the answer, but I come up empty.

"What did you do to me? I know you messed with my head, tortured me, planted your thoughts inside me, and now I think about you all the damn time. When I'm sleeping, dreaming, awake, at the most random times. What did you do?"

"I prevented you from ever feeling the pain I feel," he answers calmly and stoically, like he knew this would be my question, and he's been ready for it.

"What does that mean?"

"I made you mine, instead of his."

"Who? Julian?"

He shakes his head. "The man you think you love. I made sure that I control you instead of him."

"No," I whisper, but I know it's true. Suddenly, a rush of torture floods my mind as I remember every excruciating thing he did to me.

I look at Bishop. "You had no right! I don't care if Zeke eventually hurts me, I love him! I'll love him for as long as I can, even if it's not forever, I'll take the heartbreak later."

Bishop blinks rapidly, like something I said hurt him. Just as quickly as it flashes, it's gone.

I stalk forward, angry and needing to control my own thoughts, my own heart.

"Fix me." My voice is calm, collected, and purposeful. I don't stutter. I choose the exact words I mean.

"No," he shakes his head.

He's a liar.

This is what he wants. He wants me to beg him. He wants me to offer up everything in order to be free again.

I pause, trying to decide my next move. *Do I continue to beg for him to fix me? Getting him to give me what I want, but knowing what he could do to me is so much worse?*

Or do I back off and live with what he did to me? Missing this opportunity would cause me to betray the man I love, again, and this time in a way that I can't take back. A way that is unforgivable. A way I can't live with.

I stare down at the ring I wear on my right hand.

Bishop stares too.

"Forever doesn't exist," he says.

I frown. "Forever is as long as you want it to be. Forever can last years or for a single second. It makes no difference. The promise to love someone forever is a promise I will never break. I love him. He loves me. Our forever might be shorter than most, but we've made it this far. We can make it till the end of our forever."

Bishop walks closer, his eye on the ring. "And how many times have you already betrayed your forever?" He takes my hand, his thumb running over the ring, sending shivers through my body.

"Never," I lie.

"You can't lie to me, Siren. I know you better than anyone. I'm that voice in your head. You don't love him. You don't love anyone."

"Stop!" I yell, trying to push his voice out as I rip my hand from his.

He grins, knowing what he's doing to me.

I hold my hand against my chest, protecting the ring and my heart.

"Fix me," I say again, having to push this. This is why he's here. He wants something from me, and this is the only trade I'm going to be willing to make.

"You are fixed. When you are in love and owned by another man, that's when you are broken," Bishop says.

I shake my head and step toward him, not caring that I'm naked. Not caring how vulnerable I am. I need to be fixed. I still don't know what thoughts Bishop put into my head; I don't know how much control he has over me.

"I want to be free. I want out. I'll make a trade. You came here for a reason. You want something from me. I'll do it. Whatever it is. But get me out of here. Fix me, free me."

A slow grin forms, but his eyes continue to hide his truth. Whatever it is he wants from me will be devastating to give.

I close my eyes, taking a deep calming breath, but I know this is the right choice.

I can't be raped again.

I can't stay here.

And Zeke needs me. There is a reason he didn't come here, that he didn't save me. Zeke needs me, and that trumps everything else. Whatever I have to do, I'll do it.

"Do we have a deal?" I ask, extending my hand.

His eyes flutter down for the first time. He spots my ring, and I'm sure, my naked body. But his body doesn't harden. He doesn't lust after me.

"I'll set you free, if you do a task for me. But you'll have to come back for me to fix you," he says.

I want to argue for better terms. I want to argue for him to fix me now. I want to be free of this man—all of his darkness.

But I feel Zeke calling to me. He needs me. The most important thing right now is getting out of here. I can figure out how to kick this man out of my head later.

"Deal," I say, inching my hand toward his.

Bishop puts his hand in mine, and we shake. I just made a deal with the devil, and I don't even know what he's going to require me to do. But whatever it is, I don't care right now. I just need to be closer to Zeke.

A shockwave jolts through me though when I touch Bishop. Our eyes meet, and I know Bishop feels it too and doesn't understand. Something big just happened between us, but neither of us know what. And I'm not going to stick around to figure it out.

10

ZEKE

BEEP.

Beep.

Beep. Beep.

God, I hate that sound. I know where I am—a hospital room.

I'm alive. I should be grateful that Palmer's guards agreed to bring me here. I remember them finding us in the basement.

Palmer distraught and confused, still thinking the best thing for her was to end her life. Me barely able to move with a knife in my groin. I would have bled out in minutes if they had just left me.

"Hospital," Palmer said. *One word; one order.*

Everything went black after that. I passed out. Palmer's order must have been enough for her men to bring me here.

I don't feel any pain. I have so many drugs pumping through the IV in my arm, I could get stepped on by a five thousand ton elephant right now and I wouldn't feel it.

No one else is in the room when I open my eyes. I'm in a sterile white hospital room, with an IV pole, and a fucking beeping machine, waking me up from the depths of a drug-induced coma.

I want to rip off all the cords, the IV out of my arm, and the catheter out of my dick. I want to run away, but I'm not even sure I can sit up on my own, let alone walk out of here. Last time I checked, I could barely move my fingers.

My eyes cut down my body. I'm covered to my chest with a thick white blanket. I have no idea what's underneath. My arms are resting on top of the covers.

I grit my teeth, trying to keep the fear at bay, and then I tell my hand to move—just move. I don't care what it does —even slap myself in the face and yank the IV out.

I raise my arm.

And I exhale the fear.

I hear the door open, and a person silently walks in— not typical of a nurse or doctor entering a patient's room.

I close my eyes and still, assuming it's one of Palmer's guards coming in to check on me. I hear the heavy footprints of his steps in his boots on the floor.

I don't have a weapon. But I don't need one.

I wait patiently for him to approach my bed. He still doesn't speak—he's not going to have a chance to. I'm not becoming Palmer's prisoner again. I'm getting the fuck out of here.

His feet stop, and I attack, even though I don't have a clue if my body can still move the way I need it to.

I punch hard with one hand while I grab for his gun with the other. I swing my legs out, taking his feet out from underneath him. I watch his body fly up and then slam to ground as I aim a gun at him before I realize my mistake.

The man I just attacked is not my enemy.

"Well, I guess that answers whether or not I need to get you a wheelchair," Enzo says.

"Holy fuck," I breathe hard and fast, my body shaking as I stand over Enzo on the floor on his back. But he has a grin on his face.

I extend my hand. He takes it and is back on his feet a second later.

"Glad to know you still have plenty of fight in there." He play punches me on the chest.

"Fuck," I bite my lip as the jolt hits me like he just punched me full out.

Enzo frowns and then looks at my arm and grabs the IV lying on the bed instead of in my vein. I didn't expect the second the drugs weren't continuously running through me that I would be in this much pain.

"We have to go," Enzo says.

I nod, trusting his judgment, even though in about five minutes, ten if I'm lucky, everything Palmer put me through is going to hit me.

I grab the cords at my chest and rip them off, knowing alarms will sound as soon as I do.

"Take a breath," Enzo says.

I don't. I don't need a breath to deal with the pain.

He yanks on my catheter.

I hiss, but still have enough medication in me to avoid registering the pain.

Enzo grabs his gun from me and slips it in his pants. He starts walking toward the door. I follow and stumble from dizziness.

"Hold onto my arm," Enzo says.

I want to argue, but I won't make it out of here otherwise. I grab his arm, using him like a walker.

"Isn't this going to be suspicious, us walking out with me still dressed like this?"

Enzo opens the door. "Definitely." He grins like he did when we were teenagers and about to get into trouble.

I grin back. "Maybe I should hold onto that gun."

"No way in hell. I've always been the better shot, even when your body wasn't beat up," Enzo says.

I'm about to argue again, but he pushes us out into the hallway. I have no idea what country we are in. I have no idea what dangers await us in the hallway. *Are we going to just have to deal with fussing nurses telling me to get back into bed? Or are we going to have to fight our way out?*

Enzo already knows what to expect and is firing his gun the second we exit. I can barely keep up as he shoots down guard after guard—some of them I recognize as the men from Palmer's basement.

I regret Enzo killing them, until I see all of them had guns aimed at us.

Enzo shoots the last one in the hallway. "Come on, let's get out of here."

I nod my agreement and hobble along next to him.

"Palmer's room is on the end. Give me a minute to take her out then—"

"No."

Enzo stops and stares at me. "What? She'll come after you. She'll come after us. We can't let her live. It's not your decision to make."

"Palmer lives," I say, not budging on this.

"She can't. I won't risk my family."

"She has to live."

Enzo shakes his head. Then he grabs the bottom of the hospital gown and lifts it up. "Look what she did to you." He growls, his eyes daring me to look at my damaged body. But I don't.

I can feel all the damage. I can feel it on the surface of my skin all the way down to my bones. Unlike other times where I've been injured, I won't recover. I know instinctively that I will never have kids. I don't even know if I can fuck again.

Now isn't the time to discuss it, though.

I shove the gown back down.

"I'll do it. Just stay here," Enzo says, trying to let me go so he can kill her by himself, but I don't let go of his arm.

"No. Palmer lives. She won't come after us."

"She had dozens of guards outside both of your rooms. That seems like someone who is deep in this world."

I look back at the damage he did to the guards. "Do any of them look like career criminals? Not one of them got a shot off. And you snuck into my room without any of them noticing. They didn't have me handcuffed to the bed. They're amateurs. They are harmless even if they did come after us, but they won't because Palmer isn't a villain, she's just scared."

"What happened to you? Why are you going soft on me? She tortured you. She deserves to be punished. Death is fairer than what we would usually do to repay those sins."

My eyes glaze—Enzo's right. Most people who kidnapped and tortured me would end up getting tortured twice as bad and then eventually killed. Death would actually be showing her mercy.

I haven't changed. I would still do anything and everything to protect Enzo and his family. This just isn't one of those times where I need to protect them. There is nothing to protect them from.

I don't need revenge for what was taken from me.

I need to show compassion to a woman who lost everything and hope her pain didn't cause me to lose everything as well.

I get in Enzo's face. "I have followed your orders since we were five. I've worked for your company my entire life. I've shown devotion and loyalty to you when I could have gotten free of a mad man much sooner. So I think I've earned the right to make a decision about what to do with a woman who tortured me."

I spit out each word—my anger rumbling through my body. I'm not angry at Enzo. I'm angry at what happened to me. I'm angry I couldn't stop it. I'm angry Lucy is dead, Siren could be as well. I'm angry at what I lost.

"I saved your wife for you. Palmer lives," I say. I let go of his arm, and I start walking toward the door. I know Enzo well enough—he won't kill Palmer.

Sure enough, Enzo catches up to me, and grabs hold of my arm again as I step through the automatic sliding doors.

We won't speak about Palmer again. We've been friends too long to let a fight like this impact us. Enzo will be here for me if I ever want to talk about why, but I don't owe him a reason. He knows how serious this is to me, and that's enough.

We step out into sticky heat; we must be somewhere near the equator. It's too blazing not to be. Even hotter than in Miami.

"Which car?" I ask as I hobble down the sidewalk path toward the parking lot, not wanting to take a step in the wrong direction. Each step I take gets more and more painful.

Enzo doesn't answer me, and I look at him, standing still until he answers me.

He grins and nods in front of us. "That one."

I turn from him to the direction he's looking, and I see a van door open. I see Kai holding Siren back.

"We considered drugging Siren to keep her from

coming into the hospital with me. I knew you wouldn't want us to put her at risk to save you. Kai finally convinced her," Enzo says.

My eyes water seeing Siren alive. I can't tell from our distance whether Siren is hurt or not, but I'm thankful Enzo didn't let Siren into that hospital. I need her safe, and I didn't want her to see me so broken.

I straighten my back, trying to look like I'm not completely shattered. I let go of Enzo's arm, no longer allowing myself to use him as a crutch. But the tears, those I can't control—they pour down like rain in a thunderstorm.

"Go get your girl," Enzo says.

Siren is already way ahead of him, running toward me.

This moment is a turning point for Siren and me. I don't understand which way we are turning, but we are. I just hope we can continue to keep our promises while we change course.

11

SIREN

Bishop put me on a plane the second I agreed to his deal. It was a horrible, awful deal—one I really don't want to uphold. He'll kill Zeke in retribution if I don't keep my end of the deal, though.

Bishop freed me, now I have to do a task for him. One I don't even understand why he wants me to do.

But I don't have a choice—I have to do it.

I'm beyond ready to be done making deals with devils. I have two vows left to fulfill. Two promises stand between me and freedom.

When I look out at the grizzly looking man in a hospital gown that only hits him mid-thigh, I would make all those deals again. I would do anything to be with him.

I touch the ring he gave me. I hope to be making one more vow with Zeke soon.

Kai touches my shoulder. "Go get him." Her smile is tight and sad as she looks out at the two men we love exiting the hospital. She risked her husband's life to save the man I love.

"Thank you," I say to her through tears.

"Go," she says, pushing me out of the van. But I see her tears. Kai wants to check on Zeke as well. She wants to embrace her husband even though it's been less than twenty minutes since the last time we saw him, and this mission was on the low end of risky, compared to most of his tasks.

I jump out of the van and start running toward Zeke. I'm sore, my body aches, my inner thighs are bruised, my body has been cut, and my stomach has been queasy ever since Bishop put me on the plane to Miami to meet up with Enzo and Kai. And I've been sick the entire way here to Bogota, Columbia.

Seeing Zeke somehow just intensifies all those feelings instead of reducing them. As I run, all the fears creep back in.

Will Zeke think I'm damaged?

How hurt is Zeke?

Does he still love me?

Does he still want to marry me?

Why isn't he running toward me? Why was he using Enzo as a crutch?

Zeke takes a step toward me, and I realize why he's not running. He's barely standing on his own.

Relief fills me when it shouldn't. I shouldn't feel any happiness at his pain, but he's not running because of his injuries instead of some emotional issue between us.

I run faster, studying him closer, trying to assess his injuries, so I know where to grab him and pull him into a hug. I decide a hug is better than jumping in his arms, even though that's what I really want to do. When I see the joyous tears on his face, I know he's feeling all the same emotions I am.

Finally, I'm within reach of him.

"Be gentle with me, beautiful," Zeke says, winking at me and holding his arms out.

I jump when I know I shouldn't.

He catches me, even though his body should be too weak.

We fall onto the grass next to the sidewalk, but I'm able to turn us so I bear more of the brunt than Zeke does.

We both grunt when we hit the ground, but don't care as we are finally in each other's arms.

Zeke shakes his head. "Stop saving me." He looks pointedly at my arm where I hit the grass first. His words repeat the plea I've said to him time and time again.

Stop saving me.

I look up at Zeke with a guilty look on my face because I've been wanting Zeke to save me the entire time I was captured. I was begging for him to in my sleep, through the nightmare that was my life, but he was obviously dealing with something much worse.

"I'm sorry," I cry out, the first words I say to him.

Zeke strokes my face. "Don't. If we start with apologies, we will never stop. We have too much to be sorry for. I'm not sorry for what it took to get you back."

"I'm not either."

We grab each other in a desperate kiss. A kiss that we launch at each other with everything we've been feeling— all the pain and agony and heartbreak.

We have a lot to work through. He has no idea what I've been through, and I have no idea what he's been through. He doesn't know what happened to Lucy. He doesn't know what I agreed to get free. And I don't know what it cost him to get back to me.

This kiss is about us, though. It's about proving to the other we still love each other despite everything that has happened. Whatever it is. Whatever horrible things we've done, it doesn't matter. We love each other forever.

Zeke rolls me on top of him, and I panic when I hear the low moans he makes, but he doesn't let me roll off him. He continues to kiss me until we are both suffocating and only living on the tiny amount of oxygen between us.

Neither of us stop, though. We can't pull away. The love we feel is too much. The horrific trauma we've both been through won't allow us to stop.

"Guys, we need to get out of here before the police show up," Enzo says from behind us.

"Fuck off," Zeke says, going right back in for a kiss.

Enzo sighs. "You can keep making out in the back of the van. Just get your ass up."

I giggle and push off of Zeke. I stand as Zeke tries to keep me pressed to him, but I win and stand. I extend my hand, and Zeke takes it, but I realize that he doesn't have the strength to get himself up with my hand alone.

Enzo is already ahead of me, behind Zeke lifting his shoulders up as I pull his arm. Together, we get Zeke on his feet. Enzo throws one of Zeke's arms over his shoulders, and I do the same to Zeke's other arm.

Zeke grimaces but doesn't stop us from helping him. He doesn't really have a choice. The three of us walk back to the open van where Kai waits in the driver's seat. Enzo and I ease Zeke into the middle bench seat, lying him sideways. I climb in after him, lift his head up, and let his head fall on my lap.

I know Zeke doesn't like being vulnerable. He doesn't like looking weak. He wants to be my protector. As I stroke my hand through his long hair and think about telling him what happened to me, how he couldn't prevent it from happening, it's going to kill him. It's going to reopen every wound and make him feel inadequate.

Enzo hops in the passenger's seat, and Kai starts driving away from the hospital and Zeke's looming demons. No matter how fast Kai drives us away, the ghosts will follow. We aren't escaping them. We are just getting to a place where we can learn to survive them. A place where we can get on an equal playing field where we can fight and eventually defeat them.

I take Zeke's hand, needing to feel grounded as we drive. Zeke's hand doesn't feel warm and comforting. I don't feel whole gripping his hand, not like when we were kissing.

When we were kissing, we were able to push everything else out. The bad, the good. Every person. Every nightmare. For a moment in time, it was just us.

Now that we are in the van with Kai and Enzo, we are no longer alone. We have to face reality. Soon, we are going to have to spill everything that happened.

I'm not afraid of hearing what atrocities Zeke lived through. He's strong enough to handle his own physical pain. I don't know if he's strong enough to handle what Julian and Bishop did to me.

My grip on his hand tightens, until I'm squeezing so hard his hand turns white. Instead of telling me to let go, his thumb just traces the back of my hand gently, trying to calm me.

I look down at Zeke's eyes and see the wildness of the thoughts spinning there. We've only just begun our journey. We can say we love each other and want to spend our lives together, but our journey is going to be a lot of work. And there is no guarantee of success.

We drive all afternoon, into the darkness, before reaching the dock where the Black's yacht is tied up.

Everyone is tense as we drive, prepared for one of Palmer's team to attack us at any moment. Or waiting for Julian or Bishop to sideswipe and attack us with guns and bombs. Kai parks the rental van as close as we can get to the pier.

Zeke is pretty weak at this point. He's been dosing on and off, and he needs food, water, sleep, and possibly more medical help. There is a team of hired doctors aboard the yacht to help Zeke. The doctors saw to me when I first got on, and I trust them completely.

Zeke needs to talk to them and be examined, that is the first priority, but I can't help but think I need him. One of the most important things for us to heal is to reconnect. And that process is going to be grueling.

Kai and Enzo step out of the van, and as soon as they do, I feel a heaviness lift. It only reaffirms to me that Zeke and I need time alone to figure out where we go from here. But I'll be patient. Zeke needs medical attention first.

Enzo opens the door, and Zeke tenses. Something happened between these two in that hospital that changed the dynamic of their relationship. Enzo helps Zeke out of the van and lifts him in the air, cradling him like a baby.

"I'm carrying your big ass; you don't get to argue with me," Enzo says.

I don't hear Zeke's response, but I smile, watching the two men together like brothers.

Kai takes my hand, and we follow behind our men. Both us scanning the entire walk down the pier, watching for any of our many enemies. I try to push out one of the last times I walked down a pier, having it blown to pieces. *It won't happen again,* I remind myself.

We make it to the safety of the yacht. Enzo and Zeke have already disappeared inside the ship, but I find Nora and Beckett waiting for us.

"You okay?" Nora asks.

I nod, not able to speak.

Kai squeezes my hand, telling me she's here for me. All I want to do is snuggle up next to Zeke.

"Come on," Kai says, still holding my hand like I'm her child she's leading to her bedroom to tuck her in.

I give Nora and Beckett a small tight-lipped smile, and then I'm down in the hallways being led to the bedrooms. I expect Kai to lead me back to my bedroom and let me know the doctors are checking on Zeke. She's going to tell me to get some sleep and she'll have the doctors check on me in the morning.

Instead, she leads me to a different door. The door is already open, and I can see the doctors fussing over Zeke. I can hear Enzo's raised voice yelling at Zeke to let the doctors do their work.

"Out," Kai says forcefully.

All eyes turn to her.

"Everyone out of Zeke's room. Now," Kai says again.

I think they are all going to argue, say that Zeke needs medical attention now.

But one by one, every man files past us. Enzo gives his wife a stern look, but she just raises her brow. He leaves, letting her have all the power over the situation.

I stand behind her, still not seeing Zeke.

"Why did you do that? Zeke needs medical attention," I say, although I don't believe my own words.

"No, he needs you. Just you," she says.

She hugs me. "You have the power to heal him. Trust me." She releases me and tilts her head, telling me it's okay to enter.

"I'll have some wrapped food brought down and left outside the door. You can get it when you're ready."

I nod but don't thank her. I need to save everything for Zeke, for whatever truths are going to be spilled. Once I enter the room, I'm not going to leave again until Zeke and I have fought off all our enemies. Until we are solid in our love and our forever.

I step inside, holding my breath. I see Zeke, and my heart heals instantly, but his bleeds out to me. His heart is in turmoil—turmoil I may not be able to heal.

12

ZEKE

I'm broken.

That's what everyone's eyes have been telling me. Enzo knows how physically damaged I am. Kai knows I'm emotionally torn up. Nora and Beckett both looked at me with pity. The doctors ran into the room and treated me like I was on the verge of dying.

And then—Siren.

Siren isn't broken.

She doesn't see me as broken.

I thought what we had would be gone after what we just went through. Neither of us was able to protect the other. Neither of us was able to save the other.

We both had to fight alone.

I'm still unsure if that brought us closer together or pushed us apart—a hurricane of evil threw us to the edges of the earth. Can we ever swim the lengths of the earth to get back to each other?

"Hi," Siren says timidly, like we are meeting again for the first time. In a way, this is a second first meeting.

Her single, tentative word sends my heart racing, thump-thumping like a drum trying to call her toward me. She smiles bashfully at my need but takes her time walking to me.

She's wearing jeans and a black tank top. Her arms are fit, but I see the bruises. I see the extra layers of makeup on her face and want to know what she's hiding.

"Hi," I return sweetly.

It causes Siren to bite her lip. She chews on it like I make her nervous, in a flirtatious sort of way. Like we are two people going on our first date. I laugh at that thought because Siren and I have never even gone on a first date. Nothing about our relationship feels normal.

This moment does.

A hospital gown is the only thing hiding my secrets. Siren's wearing makeup and jeans to cover hers. This moment should be awkward. It should feel wrong. But I feel all the flutters of being in love, and I remember the last thing I said to Siren before we were ripped apart—I asked her to marry me.

I search her left hand for the ring but find it empty. My heart drops...

Siren laughs, noticing my reaction.

"What?" I ask, angry that the ring I got for her is gone.

She holds up her right hand. "Looking for this?"

"Come here," I growl.

She jumps onto the bed next to me happily like it's our wedding night instead of the night I crush her dreams. She curls into the crook of my arm, and lays her head on my chest, becoming the missing piece of my body. She fills the void taken from me, but I'm not sure if what is left of me is enough for her.

"Stop," she says.

"What?"

"Just stop. Stop thinking. Just be with me. Hold me. Love me. I love you, Zeke. Nothing that happened to either of us changed that. Nothing ever could. I still want to be your wife. I want our forever—whatever that means. I want it. I'll always love you."

I want our forever too. We never talked about what our forever means, though. *Does it mean this? We will always be running? Always be fighting? Our lives in constant danger?*

Did we want to get out? Settle down in a house with kids?

I realize now that neither of those forevers is going to work. Neither of them will allow me to love Siren the way she deserves to be loved.

I don't want a life of running and fighting, a life of danger.

But I can't offer her the kids and peaceful life she deserves either.

Siren takes my hand instead of draping her body over mine, sensing she can't be on me without hurting me, even though we haven't discussed all my injuries yet. Or hers.

She traces calming circles in my palm, and I let my thoughts go. I'm present with her. Her warmth is hugging me and reminding me what it means to be happy again.

"What do we do now?" Siren asks after we are both calmer.

I don't know. This isn't a battle against an obvious enemy. I can't just pull out my gun and take down each enemy, one after the other. Our enemies already damaged us. We both have wounds—physical and emotional. We both have pain to share and lingering feelings of anguish, of fear, of loss.

I want to draw a line and start over. Push all those feelings away and begin a new life today with Siren.

I can't, though.

She can't either.

I take her hand in mine and kiss the back of her hand. "We love. We heal—together. We take this step by step, and we find a way to defeat our demons."

13

SIREN

"Are you scared?" I ask.

"No," Zeke answers, but shudders.

"I'm terrified," I say.

"Me too." Zeke smiles tentatively. "But I don't want to be. I don't want to show you how afraid I am. This should be easy."

"No, it shouldn't be easy. It should be hard. Most couple's relationships don't survive the traumatic. Ours has been tested to the limit."

"Where do we start?" he asks.

This is too big. It's too big to just start talking and lay everything out. Separately either would be too much, but together this becomes enormous. I feel the weight on both of us, weighing us down. We have to do this.

I hear a soft rattling at the door.

Zeke turns his head and then is reaching for a gun.

It scares me that his first reaction is to reach for a gun, even though we're on a heavily guarded ship with his best friends. This time we took no precautions. We are being protected by all of Enzo and Kai's men. Over two dozen superyachts surround us with the highest level of technology. There is no safer place to be.

"It's just Kai. She said she'd leave us some food outside the door," I say, getting up. I open the door and grab the tray of food and carry it back to the bed.

"Grilled cheese," Zeke says without looking at the plate.

"Really? You think?"

He nods with a smile. "It's Kai's favorite comfort food. And she's not much of a chef. And she would have made this herself, not let the chef on board cook it."

I lift the lid, and there are two heart-shaped grilled cheeses underneath.

We both grin. "She makes such a good mom," I say.

He grabs the sandwich and takes a bite, wincing.

"Should you be eating that?" I ask.

"Probably not, but it tastes good."

I take a bite, and I moan. "What kind of cheese did she put in this?"

"I don't know, but it's delicious."

We both eat our sandwiches in quiet after that. I scarf mine down, not realizing how hungry I've been. I haven't eaten a full meal since before Zeke and I were separated.

Zeke barely nibbles on his, wincing every once in a while as the food goes down roughly in his throat. His stomach rumbles, causing him to shift on the bed. Each time he moves, I see the toll it takes on his body. I hear the cracks, the hisses, and the moans he tries to hide. I haven't seen what's underneath his hospital gown, but I know it isn't good.

"Truth or sin?" I ask, thinking maybe a simple question game will help us talk, or at least get us started.

He nods but stiffens. He's leaning against the headboard, picking at the last piece of the grilled cheese, not looking at me.

This is going to be hard.

"Truth," he finally says, his dark eyes meeting mine, begging me not to hurt him. But everything I have to say will hurt him. I start with the easiest topic to tackle. The part that is painful, but in a way we can mourn and heal.

"Lucy died." I take a deep breath and blink back the tears. Maybe starting with her death wasn't the best idea after all. My eyes find Zeke, and he doesn't look shocked. He knew. He already knew.

"Julian didn't kill her. Nor did Bishop."

He exhales a harsh, thankful breath. He was worried her death was painful.

"It was beautiful. One of the most beautiful things I've ever experienced. She died in my arms, outside, looking up at the stars and the water. Lucy was ready to die; she was at peace."

The tears sting now, remembering that moment.

Zeke pulls me to him, and we are both crying silently in each other's arms. Crying, until we drift to sleep.

———

The sun wakes us both up.

"Your turn," I start.

"I can't play. I can't do this," his throat clears.

I touch his chin, needing him to look at me so I can understand what he's saying. "You can't play? You can't be with me? What are you saying?"

"I can't play. I'm tired of playing games."

"You want me to tell you the truth? All of it?"

He nods.

"And then you'll tell me yours?"

His jaw clenches, and I know the answer is no. He wants my truth, but he doesn't want to give up his.

"No," I say.

He frowns and tries to turn away from me. I climb on his lap, and he moans loudly. I lift myself up to avoid touching him, but I'm straddling him, looking him face to face so I can get through to him.

I place my hands carefully on his shoulders to hold myself up, studying his reaction. He only flinches, so this can't be hurting him too badly.

"Why don't you want to tell me what happened to you? What are you afraid of?" I ask.

His eyes fill with tears. His teeth grind together until I can hear the clattering sound. The vein in his neck bulges. It's like he's about to burst. If he starts, it will all come out in one explosion that will obliterate us both.

"That you won't want me," he finally says.

I take his face in mine. His glorious, beautiful face. The one with as many scars as mine. He has plenty of battle wounds on his face, but it doesn't make him any less beautiful. It's part of him, as much as his dark, intense eyes, his strong jaw, and long, beast-like hair.

"I'll always want you, no matter what happened to you. No matter what you did or didn't do. It doesn't matter to me, I love you. I'll always want you."

He shakes his head like he doesn't believe me. I grab his face again and press my lips to his through the tears. I suck all his pain away with my mouth and tongue. I'm careful not to push him too far.

He can't handle getting excited and fucking right now. He needs more time to heal, and as much as we both want sex, it won't heal us right now. We need the truth, not sin.

"I'm afraid my pain will be too much for you to bear," I say, spilling my fears.

"Never." He kisses the tears on my cheeks, sucking them off the surface of my skin. "What happened to you will hurt, because once again I failed, not because I can't stand to hear it. I can handle your pain."

I shudder over him, trying not to touch him when I'm desperate to. An idea forms in my head.

"Can you get in the ocean? Will it hurt you?" I ask.

He shakes his head. "My wounds are all stitched and covered. As long as you don't expect me to swim, I should be okay."

"No swimming," I smile. "Do you trust me?"

"With my life."

"Good. What I'm asking you to do will require you to risk your life. Your heart. Your everything." I wiggle my eyebrows, trying to lighten the mood as I jump off the bed.

He chuckles at me. It's deep, but not a belly laugh, which is probably a good thing considering whatever is underneath his nightgown is going to be lots of bruises and scars and agony.

"Get ready to go for a swim."

"Siren," Zeke says in a warning word, reminding me that he can't.

I head to the door. "Trust me."

Zeke does trust me. He loves me too. And he's about to start his forever with me.

14

ZEKE

"This is crazy," Enzo says as he hands me a pair of swim trunks and a T-shirt.

I laugh. "This is the least crazy thing I've done in a long time."

"Why are you going for a swim when you should be in bed healing?" Enzo asks as he unties my nightgown.

"Because Siren wants me to."

Enzo grumbles. "That sounds like a terrible reason."

The gown falls to the floor, and Enzo gasps. He's speechless looking at me.

"I've looked worse," I remind him of the last time he came for me when I was tortured.

Enzo shakes his head. "You've been through more than all of the rest of us combined."

"I know! Why is it that I'm always the one that gets tortured the worst?"

"Because you are the biggest target."

I laugh. "And what is it about my balls? This is the second time I've been attacked there. I mean, really?"

"They are just big and hairy like the rest of you. People think they are fighting a sasquatch instead of a human."

Enzo helps me step into the swim trunks, and then he slips the shirt on over my head, like one of his twin toddlers.

"You don't have to do this just because Siren wants you to. Does she know about...?"

"No, that's why I have to do this. We need to heal. Siren has a plan to do that. I can't get the words out right now, and she can't either. This is the only way to do this. The ocean has brought us together before. It's where she found me—saved me. It won't fail us."

"I get it. But if your balls get infected and fall off, don't say I didn't warn you," he taunts me.

I nod, remembering the doctors talking about me in the hospital bed when they thought I was out of it—saying how damaged I was. There is nothing I could do to further damage my body. My scars will heal, but only the surface. Everything else will remain damaged, forever.

Forever—a promise and a curse. That's what I should have written on Siren's ring.

Enzo pats my shoulder. "You'll get through this. There was a time I thought Kai and I wouldn't survive, but we did. We figured out how to defeat our enemies and how to love each other. You will too."

"And then I brought new enemies to your doorstep."

"No, you didn't. Julian Reed was always after us. He would have come after us in a different way if he didn't find you. You actually stalled him. This is our fight, now. Not yours alone. We will destroy him like we've defeated all our enemies."

"Boys? You down there? The sun will set soon, and I'm not letting you get in the water if it's not still daylight out," Kai says from the top of the stairs and down the hallway.

"We're coming," Enzo shouts back.

Enzo helps me up the stairs, and then I see Siren preparing one of the dingy boats.

"Really? We aren't even getting in the water? Just going on a boat? I didn't need to change if that was the case," I say.

"Oh, you needed to change. That hospital gown wasn't a good look for you, big guy," Kai says.

I shoot her a dirty look.

"Just get in the boat," Siren says, happy to see me smiling and joking. She thinks it means she has a chance of healing us. The joking is just preventing me from thinking about our unsalvageable relationship. She won't want me when she knows there is no future with me.

Enzo helps me into the boat, and Siren climbs in after me. We are lowered into the water, just the two of us in the small boat.

Siren drives us about a half-mile away from the main yacht. There are several other nearby yachts, all ours protecting us, so I know we are safe. The open water is as private as we can safely be.

"You ready?" she asks.

"Since you haven't told me what we are doing, I guess I'm as ready as I can be. Although my doctors are going to lecture me about how stupid this was and how I'm risking my life."

"It will be worth it, I promise."

"I know."

She lifts her T-shirt off her head, and she's in a white skimpy bikini. The kind that displays every curve, every bruise, every cut.

"Fuck, you're gorgeous," I breathe out, but keep my hands to myself. I have too many feelings at the sight of her. I love staring at her body but hate the new unknown marks. I want her, am desperate for her. I feel the heat rise in my chest at the sight of her curves, the tightness of her stomach, her cleavage spilling out the top of her bikini. But I don't feel my cock stir. I don't get excited in my usual way.

"Down boy," Siren winks at me, thinking my problem right now is that I want to fuck her. I do. God, I want nothing more than to be able to fuck her like before. But I don't even know if I can get hard. And from the bruises on her thighs and arms, I suspect what she went through is preventing her from a romp in the sack too.

Suddenly, she's diving into the water, her body arching like I imagine an Olympic diver would move. Her ass gives me one more tempting view before disappearing under the water.

I stare down at my crotch, willing it to harden, to come to life in any way, but I feel nothing. It's like I'm numb below my waist. I know the muscles and nerves still work in my legs. I can still move, but my cock might as well not exist.

Siren's head pops up. "You coming?"

I nod and jump into the water feet first, nowhere near as gracefully as her dive into the water. This is a stupid idea; there is no way water could heal me.

When my head goes under the cool water, everything changes. I feel alive again. I feel light, like my injuries and pain no longer exist. I remember the last time we were both in the middle of the water like this. I had a bullet in my chest. I was bleeding out. I was going to die. And then...

My head pops out of the water, looking at Siren again in a new light as we both tread water.

Siren bites her lip, trying to keep her growing smile at bay as she looks at me, confident this was the right move.

"You can hold onto the boat," she says.

"No, I don't need to." I don't want to. I just want to feel the water and her.

"You're afraid. I'm afraid. But we are letting that fear go here and now."

I close my eyes, feeling the draining sun's warmth on my face, the ocean water spraying my cheeks with salt, the waves rocking us gently away from the boat. I open my eyes again, renewed. I'll never be able to thank her enough for realizing what we needed.

We will still have a lot of healing left to do when we leave the ocean, but we will have taken the first step, and the first step is the hardest.

So I open my mouth, "Siren, I—"

"Nope, you don't get to tell me anything about what happened to you yet. This is my plan." She winks at me and then takes both of my hands, holding them between us, our kicking legs keeping us above the water.

It's exhausting, but the burn in my lungs and the ache of my legs feel good. It reminds me how much I'm willing to suffer for our relationship. I just don't want Siren to suffer with me.

"Why do you love me, Zeke?"

I frown. "Are you questioning—"

"No, I just want to hear why you love me."

"We would be out here all day if I listed every reason why I love you, Siren. Way past the length of time we are able to tread water without drowning. My love for you is vaster than this ocean.

"I love you for saving me that night in the ocean; you could have easily let me drown. I know you made sacrifices that night that I still don't understand, but you took one look at me and knew I was worth saving. That I was a good man.

"I love that you are my equal, you're able to go head-to-head and toe-to-toe with me on everything. Fighting, wit, and courage. You have it all.

"I love your loyalty to those you care about. Even to those you hate. If you make a promise, you do everything to keep it.

"I love that you still want me even though I've failed you. Even though I'm not strong enough for you. I fail to live up to your equal.

"I love that you held my ex's hand all night, comforting her until she took her last breath." Tears sting again, as the pain at losing Lucy is still fresh. It haunts me that I wasn't there for Lucy, even though I know she didn't want me there. Siren was a good friend in her last moments on this earth.

"I love you because you challenge me. You're willing to fight with me, no matter how hard our life gets." My voice breaks, and I can't. I can't keep talking because if I do, I'll tell her everything that happened. I'll try to convince her she can't be with me. I'll do the right thing, and right now, I can't do the right thing. I can only do the wrong thing—love her, even though I'm going to hurt her.

I see Siren's tears, making me afraid I said the wrong thing, but then I see her smiling and laughing with such joy that her face seems to glow.

"I love you, Zeke Finn Kane. I loved you from the moment I saw you in the water. It hit me in the gut; you were different than every other man I knew in my life. You were one of the good guys, even though you had a rough exterior.

"I love that you forgave me when I hurt you, even though I didn't earn your forgiveness.

"I love that you are selfless and put your friends, even me, above yourself.

"I love how pure your heart is. With you, there is no gray —just black and white. You forgive people of their sins.

"I love your protective spirit. Even now, you are warring with yourself, trying to find a way to protect me from the darkness done to you. You think I won't love you, or I'll want out."

She pauses and lets go of one of my hands, raising her right hand out of the water. The engagement ring I gave her rests on her ring finger, along with a ring on her thumb.

"What are you doing?"

She pulls both rings off her hand and hands me her engagement ring.

"Are you giving this back?" I can't breathe. It's better for her without me, but I can't handle letting her go right now.

"No, I'm not giving it back. I'm giving it to you to put on its proper place. I know this isn't legal. Getting married in the ocean without witnesses, without a marriage license—it means nothing to the world. But to us—it means every-thing. I don't want to wait until this is over to get married. I don't want to wait until we can find an officiant and get this in writing."

I open my mouth. She needs to know what happened to me. She needs to know what she's agreeing to by marrying me, even just with us as witnesses and nothing but the ocean. If we do this, then to us, we will always be married.

"You should know before we do this—"

"No, I don't want to know what happened to you. I don't want to know what we lost, what we can't get back, what's changed. It doesn't matter. I love you as you. I love you whole; I love you broken. I love you, no matter what happens. No matter how we change. I love you forever. And

I want our forever to start now, today. I don't want to wait. I want you to know that no matter what you tell me, I'll always be your wife."

My heart heals, all the wounds stitching together. Sealing any cracks. Mending all scars. I didn't know love could feel like this. I knew it was powerful, but not enough to heal everything.

I was wrong. Loving Siren is enough to fix all of my brokenness. My physical scars will remain, but emotionally, we'll get through this.

"I, Zeke Finn Kane, take you, Siren Aria Torres, to be my wife, in sickness and in health, for richer, for poorer, till death do us part."

I take the ring and grab her left hand, slipping it on her finger.

"You promise to be my husband forever?"

"I do."

I kiss her hand over her ring.

"And I, Siren Aria Torres, take you, Zeke Finn Kane, to be my husband, no matter what happened to you or what will happen to you. No matter if our forever only lasts till tomorrow or for fifty years. No matter how many men you've killed or how many times you try to protect me but don't reach me in time to save me from pain. I take you as my husband, with all your faults, because you are worth it. I love you more than I want to take my next breath. I'm so happy that you are my husband."

I shake my head smiling, loving her unique vows.

"You promise to be my wife forever?"

"I do."

She takes my hand and the ring she was wearing on her thumb and slips it onto my ring finger. I look down at the simple silver ring that I'm sure belonged to Enzo at one point. He's going to have to fight me to get it back now.

"My anchor—forever," she says, reading the hand-done scratching on its surface.

"It's perfect."

"And now you can kiss your bride," Siren says with a smile she won't be able to wipe off her face for days.

The ocean seems to know it's time for a kiss. The waves push us together, and I kiss my wife—something I never thought I'd be doing. I never thought I could have a wife. I never thought I could put one woman above everyone else I love. But as my lips press hard against hers and the ocean pushes us harder together, solidifying our union, I'd let Enzo take a bullet every time if it meant saving this woman, my wife.

The universe in this moment may want us to be together, but I'm shaking, thinking about what I would do to protect Siren. What horrible atrocities I would commit. What lengths I would go to to keep her mine—forever.

Our forever is going to last a lot longer than a few hours or days. I want the next fifty years.

15

SIREN

WE'RE MARRIED.

Not in the eyes of any law or country, but from this moment forward, we will behave as husband and wife. I'll love Zeke as my husband. And he will love me as my wife.

We haven't discussed any of the important details couples should talk about before getting married. We didn't discuss where we'd live, or what job we would do, or if we will have kids. We had no talks about sharing our assets, staying in this dark business, or killing Julian and getting out. We didn't discuss anything.

We're married. We're committed. We will figure everything else out.

"We need to get back in the boat," I say.

Zeke nods as his limbs shake. I knew the water would heal us, even though it also has the power to destroy us. To make us so weak that physically we couldn't recover. It was a risk worth taking because the emotional wounds Zeke is carrying are deep. This was just the start—getting married in the place we started, letting Zeke know that no matter what he tells me, I'm not going anywhere.

I climb onto the boat first, and then Zeke grabs hold of the edge. I lift him over, very much like I did that first night when I met him. That night he was pretty out of it, already accepting his death, so he wasn't in pain when I pulled him over. This time though, no matter how happy he is that he married me, he's in pain. I help him lay down in the bottom of the boat.

"This was a bad idea. I'm sorry," I say.

He pants, large, heavy breaths, in and out like he just completed a hard workout instead of just treading water and being lifted into a boat.

"No, this was a perfect idea. No regrets."

"No regrets." I smile.

He shivers, and I know he's freezing. I grab towels I brought and wrap him in them. I consider telling him to take off his soaking T-shirt to help him warm-up, but I know he isn't comfortable with that yet. He wore the shirt in the water because he wasn't ready to bear his scars to me.

I won't push him, even though we are married. Healing takes time.

"Ready to head back?" I ask.

"No, not yet." He sits up slowly, wrapping the blankets around him.

"I wish I could help you warm up more," he says.

He eyes something behind me. I follow his gaze and see two thermoses. I grab them and unscrew the top of the first and take a sniff. "Hot chocolate. Kai must have packed it."

I hand it to him, and he takes it in his shaky hands before lifting it to his lips.

"Why couldn't she have packed whiskey? That would have warmed me up better than hot chocolate," he grumbles.

I grin, not that I've been able to stop since we said 'I do.'

I stare at him across from me. The sun is setting, and soon all the warmth will be gone.

"I can also help warm you up," I say, biting my bottom lip. I want him. I want to fuck him, snuggle in the bed on the yacht, and then fuck all over again.

His eyes darken, and I swear I see a momentary gaze of fear as his body language changes from relaxed shivering to hard stone.

"You okay?" I ask.

"I'm married to the most incredible woman. What do you think?" It's not an answer; it's avoidance.

It's time. Time for us both to start talking. To tell each other what happened. To rip off the bandaid.

"I was raped," I say, looking at Zeke without blinking, without showing any fear or pain. The words I just said should make me angry, should make me scared, should make me a victim—but I am not a scared victim.

"I'm sorry. I should have—"

"Stop, it's my turn to talk. Julian raped me. He did it with drugs in my system. He wanted me to want him, to give myself to him willingly. So he tricked my brain into thinking you were the one fucking me and not him."

Zeke hisses, his pain pouring through the thick air from him to me. As he does, the sun sets behind him, and we are cast into darkness. The mood changes from joy to terror.

"I'm glad he tricked me. In my head, what Julian did to me was just you. All I felt was you."

I reach across and grab Zeke's hand. "You have nothing to be sorry for because you saved me. You kept me from becoming a victim. From feeling pain. From being scared.

"Someday, I'm sure it will hit me what happened. But I don't look at the bruises now and feel angry. I don't feel like I need therapy to get through this, although I'm sure that would help. I'm still whole. Him violating me didn't ruin me. You were in my head; you were in my heart. Even though I knew it wasn't really you in me, it didn't matter because I knew you'd be waiting for me. That you would help me kill him for what he did to me.

"I'm not a victim, Zeke. So don't make me one. I'm a survivor. I still feel whole. I still feel worthy of being loved by you. I'm not mad at you that you couldn't come before Julian touched me. And I'm not going to let this weight stay with me forever."

I pause, waiting for Zeke to catch up to me. Waiting for his painful reaction. I feel his heart taking the punch my words just dealt him. I feel it hitting him over and over, and I wish I could stop his pain. I can't, though, because it's my pain.

Julian Reed didn't ruin me. He didn't take anything away from me, but he did hurt me. And it's pain we both have to deal with.

"You're a badass, and I'm so honored that you are my wife." He exhales his pain. I've never been prouder of him working through his own grief in such a healthy way.

"I love you," I whisper.

"Bishop? Did he?"

"No, he didn't rape me." I pause. "He just fucked with my head."

"How did you get free?"

"I traded a task Bishop wants me to do for my freedom. He's still in my head. He can twist my thoughts, but if I do the task and go back to him, he'll fix me."

He nods. "Will you do it?"

"Yes, for us," I answer honestly, not telling him what the task is. It's a horrible job, but I will do it for us. I don't want Bishop to control me, and he wants Zeke dead. He wants them all dead for a crime he feels they committed against him.

I need a free head, or Bishop will be able to use me against the people I love. I won't let Bishop use me to hurt Zeke.

"Do you want to know what task Bishop gave me?"

"No. I mean, I do, but I won't ask. I know you don't want to tell me. And I shouldn't know," Zeke says, knowing what I'm going to have to do will betray his friends. Now that we are married, he shouldn't stop me from protecting our marriage, even if it means I'll have to hurt our friends.

Zeke takes another long sip of his hot chocolate, and then he shrugs off the towels.

"What are you doing? You need to stay warm," I say.

"I'm plenty warm." He gives me a look, asking me to trust him. So I do.

But my heart can't stop racing, thinking about what he's about to reveal that he thinks is so bad. That he thinks will make me stop loving him.

"Lucy's lover, Palmer, was the woman who took me. She took me because she was in pain. She was angry Lucy was dying, and she couldn't stop her death."

"Lucy loved her, until her dying breath," I say.

Zeke nods. "They both did. If you want to know what we are capable of doing for love—this is what we are capable of."

Zeke removes his wet shirt over his head, and I see every mark on his body. His body is more black and blue than it is healthy flesh. The parts that aren't bruised are stitched or bandaged, indicating wounds. His chest is the worst I've seen it. Once he heals, there won't be a part of him that isn't scarred.

He stands up, and I feel queasy, afraid of whatever comes next.

He lowers his swim trunks until he's naked before me in the darkness of night. The moonlight illuminates his body, showing me all of him.

If I thought his chest was bad, his legs are worse, and his manhood—it's swollen, red, and damaged.

This is what he was afraid of. This is what he was terrified of revealing to me. That he might be too damaged to ever make love to me again. Too damaged to ever have a chance at us having kids. Too broken.

This is what our love is capable of. This is the type of damage we could inflict on the world, on others we love in order to protect our love—our marriage.

It should terrify me. It should pain me. It should make me feel so many horrible things. Instead, all I see is a man I love. A man I will always love. A man whose love will stay with me forever.

I open my mouth to tell him that, but my stomach can't hold back anymore. I grab the boat and vomit over the side, knowing Zeke is going to see this as a bad sign. He's going to think I'm disgusted by him, even when that couldn't be further from the truth.

16

ZEKE

Siren's reaction to my body is straight out of my nightmares. I don't know how it could have been worse. She got physically sick at the sight of my disgusting body. I look like a hideous monster.

Sure, my face looks the same, but underneath my clothes, I'm covered with ugly scars twisting over all of my skin. And that part of me that she should be most attracted to is a mangled mess.

Letting her marry me without the truth was a mistake. *What was I thinking? I'm an idiot.*

"We can take it back. We aren't married. We had no witnesses. We didn't sign any papers. We can take it all back." I move to remove the ring as I sit back down, the chill in the air no longer affecting me. All I care about is Siren's reaction.

"No!" she practically screams at me.

"I don't want you to feel obligated to be married to me when you aren't even attracted to me."

She vomits again, and I wince. She's not even looking at me anymore, and she's throwing up her disgust.

"Just—one second," she says.

That one second lasts a lot longer than just one second. In that second, Siren must be regretting her decision to marry a beast like me. We were both raped, both violated. But she came out whole, at least physically, and I came back looking like an alien to her. I look nothing like I did before.

She starts dry heaving, and I can't wait anymore. I move to her, stroking her back, trying to help her to relax even though I'm sure my touch isn't helping. I grab a towel from the floor and wrap myself again so she won't have to look at me.

I hand her the hot chocolate to try and wash out her mouth, but she just shakes her head. I wish I had more to offer her.

Her beautiful eyes sparkle as she looks at me. "I've never been more attracted to you, Zeke. We are absolutely not taking back our vows. We are married. We will always be married. Don't you dare take that back or ruin that moment for me."

I blink. "You can't be attracted to me."

She grabs my hands again. "I am. Being attracted isn't just about the physical. I'm attracted to your physical prowess, sure. I will always love your long hair and curse you to hell if you ever cut it off. But I'm also attracted to your strength. Your courage. Your love for me."

"Then, why did you throw up? I don't understand your reaction."

She purses her lips, breathing again like she's about to be sick again. She holds up a finger, asking me to wait another second.

Goddamn, I can't wait. There is a reason she didn't list patience as a reason she loves me.

"Siren? What is it? What's wrong?"

"I'm pregnant."

My whole world stops—not in a bad way. Not in an 'I've just been shot, and my body is broken and weak, and I can't move' kind of way. My heart skips, my ears tell me I must have heard her wrong, and my breath is swept away.

"How? I mean...really? You're pregnant?" I try to hide the hope in my voice, but it's there. I can't give her a baby. I know it without a doctor confirming it. I've seen the mangled parts hanging between my legs, and there is no way those parts will work properly ever again. But this—this could give us everything. This could give us the kid I instinctively know we both want, even though we've never spoken about it.

Her face brightens at my reaction, and she walks over to me, trying to find a way to sit next to me on the small bench next to my giant ass.

"I don't want you to get too excited. I haven't taken a test, and I haven't had a doctor confirm it yet either. So I might not be—but it's just a very educated guess after knowing my body so well," she says.

Calm down, I tell myself. Don't get too excited. Not until it's confirmed by a dozen doctors. Not until she's gotten through the first trimester. But there is no stopping my excitement.

I grab Siren and jerk her onto my lap.

"Zeke! No, I'll hurt you."

"Not possible, not after that incredible news."

"So, you're happy?"

"I'm ecstatic!" I grab her lips, capturing them with my own, trying to get them to stop grinning long enough to give her a proper kiss. Instead, we both just end up laughing and smiling like idiots against each other's lips.

"I was nervous you didn't want kids. I wasn't even sure I wanted kids, but then I saw Kai and Enzo's twins and—"

"And everything changed. The impossible became possible. If they can do it and keep their kids safe, then so can we," I finish her sentence.

She nods, leaning her head against my chest, her hand going to her still flat stomach. I put my hand on top of hers.

"I've never felt this happy. I never thought I'd be married. Never thought I'd have kids. Never thought I'd be happy. I thought I'd die one day protecting Enzo's ass."

Our smiles stop at that. This changes everything. I mean, sure, the getting married part changed a lot, but the having a kid confirmed it. There is no going back. Our family comes first—the three of us.

"I can't protect them anymore, can I?" I ask.

Siren frowns. "I don't know. We have to put each other first. Which means we won't be doing as good of a job at protecting our employers, our friends. I don't think Enzo and Kai are just going to let you stop working for them. Not because they are cruel, but because they love you and want you in their life."

I brush my hand through her wet hair, lost in thought.

"I love you, Zeke. Everything else we will just have to figure out," she says, pressing a tender kiss against the hardness of my neck.

I stare down at her white bikini and see her nipples harden as she leans against my bare chest.

"Let's head back and stop thinking about our future. At least, what this means for our future in this world. Let's just think about the three of us and enjoy our wedding night," I say.

"Agreed," Siren says. She moves to get off my lap to start

the boat up, but I can't let her go. I don't know if I can ever let her go again.

Instead, I'm able to lean back enough to start the engine and steer us back to the yacht.

We tie up at the aft, and then Siren climbs off my lap with a towel draped over her shoulders. Enzo is waiting on the yacht's platform, ready to help me out of the boat and probably to try and tuck me back in my bed.

"I love you, Enzo, like a brother, but I'm naked, and it's my wedding night, so if you'd like to be able to look at your kids in the morning without a black eye, I suggest you go back to bed," I say.

Enzo raises an eyebrow. "As if you could beat me up in your state."

I grab onto the railing and pull myself onto the yacht. The towel around me drops to the floor, and I'm naked standing on the yacht.

"I beat you up in the hospital no problem," I say.

Enzo rolls his eyes and then looks to Siren. "You okay dealing with this ogre tonight, or do you need help?"

"I got this," Siren smiles brightly.

Enzo nods. "I'll keep the happy news from Kai until morning, but expect some extravagant over-the-top celebration in the morning. The twins get up at six. I'll see you at seven."

And then Enzo is gone.

"Bastard," I curse. I pull Siren into my arms. "There is no way I'm going to be done with you by seven."

Siren giggles as I try to scoop her up in my arms and fail.

"Dammit, this isn't very romantic, is it? I can't even lift you up and carry you over the threshold like I want to," I say.

She gets a twinkle in her eye.

"Whatever you are thinking, no," I grumble.

But before I can protest, she's scooped me up in her arms and is carrying me down the stairs to our bedroom.

"This is really emasculating; you know that, right?"

"I do, and I don't care. We are equals in this marriage. Most men don't get the pleasure of having their wives carry them over the threshold, but how lucky are you?" She kicks the door open and plops us down on the bed.

"You're incredible; you know that? The strongest, most badass woman I've ever had the pleasure of knowing. I never thought I'd get married, but if I had to imagine the perfect woman, she wouldn't even come close to comparing to you. I thought I wanted a woman who would drag me out of this world, not one who could fire a gun and throw a punch as easily as I can. But I was so wrong."

"You didn't live up to the guy I pictured as the man I wanted to marry," she says.

I frown.

She grins. "Kidding—of course, you're better, hubby."

"Better than your first hubby?"

She makes a disgusting face. "I was only married to him on paper. It wasn't real."

"And us?"

"We aren't legal on paper, but we are real in all the ways that matter. And tomorrow, I'm going to shout to the world that we're married."

My eyes heat, and I lick my lips in anticipation of tonight. I roll her over onto her back as I prop myself up on my elbow next to her. I don't have the strength to give her an entire night of making love to her body like I want, but I have enough to make her feel good on her wedding night. To give us memories we can keep when things get hard.

"What are you doing?" she giggles, but her voice falls serious when I throw the towel lying lazily on her body to the floor.

"I'm making love to my wife."

"Zeke, I love you, but I don't think this is the best id—" her voice stops when I kiss her neck just above her collarbone. It's tender and sweet, and she makes gasping noises when I do it. Her body curls, her back arches, her hips shift. She can say this isn't a good idea all she wants, but it's the best idea.

"You have to tell me if I do anything that..." I can't finish my sentence. I'm too scared that if I even mention what Julian did right now, it will be enough to ruin the moment.

She looks up at me with hooded lids and a soft expression on her face, like she already came and we are about to begin round two, instead of just starting.

"All I'm thinking about is you, Zeke."

I take a deep breath, realizing I'm the one who's terrified. My biceps are shaking, not from the fatigue of holding myself up, but because if I touch her wrong, she'll be back in that moment with Julian, that moment I couldn't save her.

"Make love to me, Zeke. Put your mouth all over my body."

That's all I need. I kiss her neck again, loving how it makes her squirm. I wonder if I could make her come if I stayed at it long enough. But I'm not patient enough to try, and I want to explore her entire body.

I pull on the string at her neck that releases her bikini top, and then I shove the thin white fabric away. I kiss over the upper curve of her breast before finding her nipple, so ready to be devoured.

I take my time, enjoying every sound. I've been selfish

when I fucked her before—teased her to get her excited for when my cock finally entered her. But tonight isn't about me. Tonight is all about her.

I'm going to memorize every sound, every whimper. I'm going to know which spots on her body are her favorites, and which cause her toes to curl.

I take her nipple, licking a slow circle around it before biting it gently with my teeth. I won't be rough with her tonight. Not for a second. I don't want to induce any bad memories.

The gasp followed by the torturous whimpering tell me I could definitely make her come by just stimulating her nipples, but it's not what I want. I want all of her body.

I give both of her nipples ample attention, until they're so hard they could cut through ice. Then I kiss down her scarred stomach. I kiss each scar, and wonder at the thought that there is most likely a baby in there. Tomorrow, we will find out for sure. There are doctors on board. I'm sure they can run a simple pregnancy test.

Siren strokes my hair as I take my time kissing her stomach. It's not turning her on like when I was torturing her nipples, but I need a moment to gather myself so I don't end up crying like a virgin bride on her wedding night.

All it takes is spotting how soaked her white bikini bottoms are to remind me of my mission.

"Remove these, and then ride my face," I say in a deep, commanding voice. I feel my body shaking, even kissing over her body is taxing right now. But I can lay on my back and fuck her pussy. My tongue has plenty of stamina for that.

I lay back on the bed, not covering my own nakedness even though I don't want Siren to see me as her injured anchor. I want her to see me as her knight in shining armor.

I want her to know that from now on, I'll move mountains, change the flow of rivers, and jump across oceans to protect her and our baby.

I look over at Siren, now a naked goddess coming out of the water, much like she was the first day I met her. Her hair is still soaked and parted. Her entire body glows from the saltwater, still sticking to her skin combined with my kisses, bringing her blood to the surface of her skin.

"I should have called you goddess, not Siren," I say. "Although, it was your fault I call you Siren."

She grins. "Siren fits better." She carefully parts her legs over my face, not lowering herself yet, but damn, do I have a good view. Her drenched pussy. Her flat stomach. Her gorgeous breasts. "If you thought of me as a goddess, you wouldn't remember that I can lure you to your death as easily as I can save you."

I grab her hips. "Oh, I know my Siren. I know. That's one of the many reasons I love you." And then I yank her down onto my face. I taste how sweet she is, mixed with the saltiness of the ocean.

"Jesus, Zeke. Keep that up, and I'm going to come in like five seconds," Siren purrs as she grabs the headboard above my head as she rocks her hips back and forth, increasing the friction. I circle my tongue over her clit, knowing she likes the unexpected. I switch my technique up again, from fast to torturously slow. The adorable cry of a whimper tells me I'm doing it right.

I smile. "I need to feel you pulsing around me when you come."

I slip a finger between her folds and into her depth. I feel how wet, warm, and perfect she is. She pulls me in deeper, deeper, deeper. So deep I never want to leave. And I never will.

I hear her scream my name, but it seems like she's in another room shouting my name. It's distant, not right above me.

Everything feels isolated for a moment.

Not because I don't hear and feel everything she's feeling, but because I'm hyper-focused on my own body for a second. I can definitely be a selfish, cocky bastard.

But this isn't just about me. It's about our future.

Taking my wife like this, bringing her so much pleasure, hearing her come apart above me has done something to my body. I feel a stirring I never thought I'd feel again—a warmth between my legs, a hardening.

Just like that, I have hope for our future again.

17

SIREN

"How am I sore, and you didn't even fuck me with your cock?" I ask, stretching as Zeke kisses my neck, trying to get me all hot and bothered for the fourth time since we became man and wife.

He grins. "Because my hands can stretch you as well as my cock can."

"Ahh," I moan as his fingers slip between my legs again.

He's made me come three times already, which may not be our high score for a night, but it was exactly what we needed last night. Each time would end with me coming and then snuggling up in Zeke's arms as we drifted off to sleep with the smell of me on his breath.

Each time he made me come, I'd sneak a peek at him. I'd study him, trying to read all the signs he's not telling me.

I'd notice how his voice changed.

How his nipples would harden, along with all the muscles on his chest.

How his face would flush.

Maybe it was wishful thinking, but I know his cock started to harden and lengthen that last time. We need to talk to a doctor to understand his injuries and his road of recovery. But it sparked hope—hope that he can heal. That nothing was taken from him. And that not only are we going to be blessed with a baby, but we are going to be a fully functioning family.

"We need to get you a pregnancy test. I'm dying to know for sure," Zeke says, still moving his fingers over my clit before dipping them inside me.

"Mmmm," is all I can manage to get out. I'm sure he's right, whatever he's talking about. I would agree to anything he says right now.

He laughs, realizing now is not the time to have an important conversation.

Two seconds later, I'm coming and screaming, lost to my own pleasure. I really want Zeke to heal so I can fuck his cock again. But if for some reason that's not possible, I won't be missing out on the pleasures of the world. He makes sure of it. I will just have to figure out how to make him feel this good while we are waiting for him to heal.

There is a loud knocking, and we both growl at the door grumpily.

"Wake up, sleepyheads! Although, I know you're already awake. I heard Siren moaning," Kai says from our bedroom door.

"I thought the room was soundproof?" I ask Zeke.

"It is! Well, mostly, but there are security cameras every-where, and I might have checked it out this morning just to see if you were awake before I came down," Kai says, opening the door.

"Privacy. Boundaries," Zeke hisses at her.

She shrugs. "I know, I know. I'm sorry. I'm just so excited to have a sister!"

Zeke looks from the crazy woman invading our room to me. "You aren't sisters."

"Sure, we are. You're married. And you and Enzo are practically brothers. And you and I are like brother and sister. Either way, it makes her my sister-in-law now!"

Zeke narrows his eyes at Kai like he's going to murder her. "What's happened to you? You are never this bubbly. That's why you and I get along so well."

"Sorry, I had an extra shot in my coffee this morning. Enzo has me drinking cappuccinos now, and I get a little too excited sometimes. But I'm just really, really happy! I have my family back!" Kai comes around to my side of the bed and hugs Zeke, then leans over him to hug me.

I try not to blush as we are both naked and smell like sex, but I guess Kai watched us on the security camera too, so I shouldn't be embarrassed about the smell.

"The first thing I'm doing when I get out of this bed is disabling the security cameras in this room and changing the lock so you can't get in," Zeke grumbles.

"I didn't watch anything, you perv," Kai says, winking at me. *She definitely watched something.*

"Now, get up and get dressed. I want to hear all the details about your wedding and plan something where we can celebrate all our marriages. Enzo and I didn't get to have a wedding with all our friends either. But now you're here, and we can."

"You do realize there is a mad man after us, right? You shouldn't be this happy," Zeke says, but he has a smile on his face now. He's happy for his friend.

"Just get up and get dressed, you oaf. I'm tired of looking at your ugly ass. I've been dealing with unmarried, single guys who only want to talk sports and guns. I'm ready to talk girly stuff, so get up so that Siren and I can become bestest friends."

I smile at that. "You are going to have to fight Nora on that one."

"Oh, I know. I haven't told her that you got married yet because I know she's going to want to be your maid of honor when you do a redo, but I get to be best man, right? You're not going to make it Enzo or Langston?"

"Get out! Or you're going to see more of my naked ass than you've ever wanted to," Zeke growls.

Kai leaves, and Zeke stares at me. "Sorry about her."

I grin. "She just loves you and is excited for you. If you think she's bad, just wait until Nora finds out. She's going to want a re-enactment of the wedding and last night's activities."

He frowns. "I think we should just barricade ourselves in this room and never leave."

My stomach growls.

He presses his hand to my stomach. "I guess we should feed the little guy."

I smile and press my hand over his. "Probably."

"Any chance we can sneak away and find a doctor to administer a pregnancy test without everyone on board speculating or knowing you might be pregnant?"

"Well, we need to get you checked over too, so after breakfast, we'll go see one of the docs on board, and hope they have a pregnancy test. If they don't, we may have to tell Kai or Enzo to stop the yacht somewhere to pick one up."

"Those doctors better hope they have a pregnancy test, or I'm throwing them overboard."

"Says the man who can't even lift me."

"That's it! You're going to get it!" He grabs me and starts tickling me, and I've never been happier that he's able to overpower me. It means he's feeling better and getting some of his strength back.

When we can't laugh anymore, we both get dressed. We both want to shower but decide we don't want to piss off Kai and Nora for making them wait, so we just put on clothes. Zeke struggles to put on his jeans, but I know he's determined to not let his injuries affect him in any way. So if he wants to wear jeans, then dammit, I'm going to support him wearing jeans.

We hold hands as we walk upstairs and into the kitchen, following voices. All eyes fall on us, and the room goes quiet as Kai, Enzo, the twins, Nora, and Beckett all stare at us.

"Well, are you going to announce the news or am I?" Kai asks, grinning from ear to ear.

"Ugh, like you haven't already told everyone, woman," Zeke grumbles with a smile.

Kai rolls her eyes. "I have not told anyone."

"You marry," Ellie says.

The room erupts in laughter, revealing Kai to be the liar that she is. Kai scoops up her little one from the high chair and snuggles her, rubbing Ellie's leftover breakfast all over her white shirt and not caring one bit.

"That was supposed to be our secret, little one," Kai says, kissing her chubby cheeks. She looks at Enzo, who must be able to read his wife better than I can. Suddenly, there are champagne flutes in all of our hands.

"I want to toast the happy, married couple," Kai says. "To Siren and Zeke. We are so happy you found each other, and we look forward to being able to celebrate your love today and forever. We can't wait until you have lots of babies for us all to raise together." Kai winks at me like she knows I'm pregnant. She can't know when I don't even know for sure.

"To Siren and Zeke," the group rejoices.

We all clink our glasses, and I take a minuscule sip to not raise suspicions.

"I can't believe you got married without me there! I was supposed to be your maid of honor, you bitch," Nora says, pulling me into an obnoxious hug.

"Well, it was sudden, and you know, not legal or whatever, so I'm sure if we ever decide to make it legal, we'll invite you to be our witness at the courthouse," I say.

Nora pulls back, looking at me like I'm crazy. "Kai and I will not allow our best friends, who have survived death and murdering devils, to have their love celebrated in a courthouse. When you get married legally, we will be doing it in a big way! Kai and Enzo didn't get to be married in front of those they loved, either. So it can be a joint wedding or a doubleheader or something! I'm so excited!"

I laugh. "Slow down." I squeeze Zeke's hand who looks at Nora like she's insane. "We haven't agreed to a big wedding. We already had everything we wanted. And we can celebrate today."

"Fine, fine. Let me see the rings, though!" Nora grabs my hand around my champagne glass. "Love it! It's so you. You're not a diamonds kind of girl."

"No, I'm not."

"Zeke, let's see it," Nora says.

"It?" Zeke asks, obviously oblivious to my friend's conversation.

"Your ring." Nora grabs his left hand and studies it closely. "It's perfect!"

"It is," Zeke says, bringing my hand to his lips to kiss me, which only eggs Nora on.

"We should have a dance tonight! Everyone could get dressed up, and we could have a wedding reception! Oh my god! I'm so excited," Nora says.

"Are you going to dance with Beckett? He hasn't stopped looking at you," I whisper, wondering how they are doing together.

She sighs. "No, I'll be a single lady going home alone, but it could still be fun. Beckett doesn't seem interested in dating, fucking, or anything fun."

I kiss her on the cheek. "Your happily ever after is coming."

"I know."

Kai comes over, holding Ellie.

"Ooh, give her to me," Nora says, grabbing the toddler and turning from us.

"Congrats, you guys!" Kai hugs us both, and then she whispers in my ear. "It's just grape juice, just in case..." She winks again.

I'm blinking rapidly, shocked she's figured out I might be pregnant.

"I'm right, aren't I?" Kai asks, studying me closely.

Zeke narrows his eyes. "Right about what?"

"Right about everything," Enzo says from behind her. "Congrats, you two."

"Yes, congrats. I know we haven't spoken about how you tried to kill me a while back, but you two make a good fit. I'm really happy for you. And I'm sorry I couldn't rescue Siren, I—" Beckett says awkwardly.

"It wasn't your fault. It was mine. No need to apologize," Zeke says, forgiving Beckett for not being to rescue me just like he couldn't.

"Thank you," I say to everyone trying to move away from the depressing turn Beckett and Zeke started down. "But we don't really have to celebrate."

"We do," Kai and Nora say at the same time.

Zeke and I sigh at the same time.

"So am I right?" Kai leans in so only I can hear her.

"I don't know. But I'd find out a lot sooner if we weren't having to have a weird wedding party breakfast and could meet with a doctor or get a pregnancy test," I hiss back, careful not to raise my voice.

"I can help with that!" She turns to the room. "Alright, enough fussing. Zeke needs to get checked out by a doctor, and we need time to discuss a redo wedding for all of us."

Enzo frowns. "We haven't even eaten the breakfast you cooked yet. Shouldn't we all eat together? Zeke can see a doctor—"

But Kai throws him a look, and he shuts up.

"I'll bring the breakfast to you two later," Kai says.

"I'm sure you will." Zeke fires a warning look at her. If she comes into our room unannounced or looks at the security camera again, he's going to throw her overboard.

"The code is 5523," Kai says.

"Wait, you are giving them our bedroom? What's wrong with theirs?" Enzo asks.

Kai gives him another look, and he shuts up again. She leans into me. "Under the sink on the left. I'll have the doctor come up for Zeke in twenty minutes."

I nod and pull Zeke away from everyone toward Kai and Enzo's bedroom.

"Why did Kai give you access to her bedroom?"

"She has a pregnancy test under the sink."

"Oh."

"Yea, oh." A million little butterflies flutter in my belly, quickly turning into rabbit-sized butterflies hopping around, causing me to jump nervously as we walk.

"Are you feeling okay?" Zeke asks.

"Yep."

"Me too," he says, just as nervous as I am.

We get to the door, and I have to enter the code three times to gain access, but finally, the door opens.

We walk straight to the bathroom. I lean under the sink and pull out the pink box that has one pregnancy test left in it.

I let go of Zeke's hand reluctantly, and then go pee on the stick.

"How long do we have to wait?" I ask, laying the test on the counter.

"Three minutes," Zeke answers, staring at the pregnancy test like it holds our entire future.

It does, which makes this moment so terrifying. This might be our only chance to have a baby that is biologically both ours. Any other kids we have might be adopted, or only me and some sperm guy. This could be our only shot at having something that is part of both of us.

Zeke never asked me if I thought the baby was his or was a result of Julian raping me, but the timing doesn't work for the baby to be Julian's. I know it's Zeke's, but I'm glad I don't have to confirm it to Zeke in that way.

Staring at the test makes me just as nervous to learn I am pregnant as scared to learn I'm not. I'm not sure I would make a good mom. I'm not sure bringing a baby into my world is a good idea, not when I'm constantly being shot at. I'm not the kind of person our kid could look up to. I've done horrible things, things I can't explain to a kid.

Zeke puts his hand in mine, and suddenly it doesn't matter that I don't have all the skills it takes to be a good mom. Zeke is going to make a great dad—he will fill in the holes I'm lacking and vice versa. Together, we will make great parents, and this baby will be loved. That's what matters.

18

ZEKE

WE'VE TURNED INTO A CRYING, SOBBING MESS. I DON'T THINK we are ever going to stop crying or smiling. Nothing can ruin this moment. This moment has stretched into twenty minutes of just holding and laughing and crying and smiling—pure joy. I've never felt anything like it, but I can only imagine holding my baby in my arms for the first time will be the only thing able to top finding out that my wife is pregnant.

"I can't believe I got a wife and baby in the same day," I say.

She laughs. "You don't have the baby yet. He or she still has another seven or eight months until you meet him or her."

I grab her stomach and kiss it again for the hundredth time. "Nope, mine, now."

There is a knock on the door, and we both quickly grow solemn. Kai said she'd send a doctor in to examine me after we had a few minutes alone, but right now, I want this moment to last forever.

"We can celebrate more after, but we need to know the good and the bad," Siren says.

I nod. Siren takes my hand, and we exit the bathroom and open the door together.

"I'm Dr. Rancor," the gentleman in his fifties says.

"Zeke," I say, shaking his hand. "This is my wife, Siren."

He shakes her hand as well. "Pleasure to meet you both. Mrs. Black has given me a general overview of your condition, but I'd love to do a full examination and hear from you so I can best help you."

I nod as he enters the room with his bag of equipment. He sits in a chair, while Siren and I sit on the edge of the bed. And then I tell my story, while Siren and the doctor listen intently to every word. I didn't think I could talk about it so easily, but finding out I'm going to be a father soon seems to make me brave and push any other emotions away.

"So what do you think? Am I going to be able to fuck again? Have more kids?" I don't mince my words. I want to know the truth.

"Well, we won't know until I examine you. If you could remove your clothes," the doc says.

I do as he says, but my mind isn't on me. It's on Siren. "What do we need to know about the first trimester? I know Siren has been having some morning sickness. What else?"

The doctor chuckles. "First-time parents?"

"Yes," we both say anxiously.

He laughs. "Well, I'm not an obstetrician, so my experience is limited, but for now, unless you are feeling really sick, eat healthily, take it easy, get plenty of rest, and let your body do the rest."

I frown, not liking his answer. I spend the next ten minutes drilling him about everything. Every symptom Siren could have. Every sign of danger we should look for and what to do about it. What we should know about giving birth, especially if we happen to be out at sea on a yacht. When do we really need to get to a hospital? I've picked the doctor's brain of everything I can think of by the time he's finished examining me.

"Well?" Siren asks as I get dressed.

"I wish I could give you all the answers as easily as explaining what to expect while you're expecting," he smiles briefly. "But we just don't know how he will heal or what damage has been done. I would say the initial swelling has gone down. The wounds have more or less healed. You are welcome to try having sex when you feel up to it, but there are no guarantees in medicine or in life. The doctors did a good job stitching you up, but that's all they did. It's hard to know what's going on beneath the surface. Only time will tell."

I frown, and Siren takes my hand, not liking that we got no answers.

"I'll give you the number of the best plastic surgeon and urologist I know in case you need it. But you won't get answers until you try."

"Thank you, doctor," Siren says, leading him out while I sit back down, frustrated.

"You okay?" she asks.

I nod.

"Well, at least he didn't say there was no hope. We have hope and permission to try, so when the time is right, we'll try."

She takes my hand again. "Come on, let's go celebrate with everyone and share the good news."

An hour later, after celebrating, Enzo and I go up to the security room like we used to to get away from everyone. I feel bad about leaving Beckett with the women, but as much as Nora says Beckett isn't interested, he sure does look at her a lot, so I don't feel too badly.

"First things first, block security camera access to my room. And change the code so Kai can't get in," I say.

Enzo laughs but does as I say.

"We need to talk about Julian and Bishop. We have to take them out. We have to destroy them," I say.

Enzo nods. "We do. But Kai and Siren will both want in on the conversation. And we will need Langston and the whole team to take them down."

"Siren stays out of this. She can be involved in the planning, but that's it."

"She won't like that, or agree to it," Enzo says.

"She will."

Enzo studies me closely. "Siren's pregnant."

He doesn't ask it like a question. "Kai told you?"

He shrugs. "Just a guess. That's the only reason I can think of that Siren wouldn't get involved in a fight and you would be that confident she would sit out of a fight."

"Yea, she's pregnant. We were going to wait and tell everyone, but Kai already guessed, and I'm sure she's down there spilling the beans to everyone else."

"That's my wife and your bestie. She can't keep a secret as good as this one. Although, I'm still pissed she didn't tell me you were alive."

I sigh. "I guess it's good everyone knows. Then we can keep Siren safe."

Enzo nods. "We have a timeline now. We need this mess dealt with before the baby comes. Then we can get back to our usual work."

I shake my head, realizing in this moment exactly what my future holds.

"No."

"No?"

"I mean, yes, we need to kill Julian and Bishop, the sooner, the better. But I won't keep working for you after. After they are dead, I want out. I want a life where my kids can grow up without being afraid."

"My kids are growing up without fear. You can have this life. This life with your friends, your family, and still have kids."

"No, I can't."

Enzo frowns. "Think about it. You aren't going to be happy becoming a security guard at some mall and coaching your kids' soccer games on the weekend. Siren isn't going to be happy as a stay at home mom or wait-ressing at some local cafe."

"You think those are the best jobs we can get?" I smirk, knowing he's joking.

"You both need a job that involves doing what you love. Wielding a gun, throwing punches, kicking ass, and protecting others. You need this life more than Kai and I do."

I shake my head. "You're wrong. Siren and I don't need this life. And we won't be able to do a good job once we have kids. Once we do, everything changes. We will put our family first—over you, over whoever we're working for, and over anyone else we're supposed to protect."

"I'd never ask you to protect me over your own family."

"I know, but that's the only way I'd work for you. If I'm going to continue to be one of your guards, I need to be able to take a bullet for you. Having a family means I won't."

Enzo nods, understanding spreading on his facial features. "Well, think about it. Kai isn't going to let you go easily. And I'm guessing, neither is Siren."

I turn back to the screen that holds all the information we have on Julian, which is a lot. We have very little on Bishop, which scares me.

"Let's figure out how to kill these guys and protect our families. One last time—together."

19

SIREN

"Time is up, Siren," Bishop whispers sin into my ear. He knows I don't have a choice but to do what he wants. I can't live like this forever. I can't be controlled forever. I can't.

"No, I need more—more time. I can't do this yet."

"You have to. The time is now."

"No, you never gave me a deadline. You just said to do it, but never when. It's too soon."

"Siren," his voice is a warning. A threat that he will keep getting into my head every night, every morning, every hour until I do what he wants. Until I can't push him out of my head anymore. Until, even when I'm kissing Zeke, I'm thinking about Bishop.

"I need more time. Just a little longer. Please."

He shakes his head in the dark, or maybe those are shadows. I can't tell if he's really here or he's just tricks on my mind. Either way, I need him gone; I'll do anything to rid myself of him.

"Are you dreaming about him?" he asks.

"Who?"

"Julian."

I pause. "No, Julian's not in my head."

"Good, don't give him another thought."

"I have to. You know what I owe him. It's as bad as what I owe you."

He shakes his head. "Let me worry about Julian. You just focus on my task. Do as I say, complete your task, and you'll be free of more than one man."

"I don't trust you. If I do this, you'll fix me?"

He smirks. "Do this and I'll more than fix you. I'll set you free; your heart will be yours again."

"But I don't want—"

"Enough. Of course, you want to own your own heart. Don't give it away. Don't let Zeke or any other man take it. It's not theirs. It's yours."

My lips thin into a frown. I don't understand why Bishop always tries to give me relationship advice.

"I'm married," I say.

He pauses, and I can tell what I said shakes him. Not because he wants me, like Julian does, but because he has something against committed relationships.

"All the more reason to do this now."

No.

I don't speak the word. It's in my head. I don't say the word, because I know it isn't true. I'll do the task Bishop gave me; I need him out of my head. I need him gone forever. If doing this one task will get him out, then so be it.

My eyes fly open, and I gasp into the darkness of the room. Bishop's gone. I'm in bed with Zeke, who is snoring adorably next to me.

It was all a dream. Bishop isn't really here. He's not in my head.

I stand up and head to the bathroom to get a drink of

water in my panties and tank top. My hair is a disheveled mess, but it has nothing on the nerves shooting through me.

I remember what Bishop wants. I remember what thoughts he's put in my head if I fail. But this task he wants me to do, it's too much. It might not even work.

I grab the cup next to the sink, turn on the faucet, and fill it. But I don't drink the water. I slam the glass down on the counter, watching the glass chip.

I push air quickly through my nostrils, trying to calm the fuck down.

No, it will work. I know what Bishop wants, and I know exactly how to do it. Bishop knows me well. Possibly better than any other man—even Zeke. He's figured out my head, my thoughts, everything.

I wish I could fail. I wish I didn't have the skills to do the task Bishop gave me. If I tried and failed, that would be fine. I would have done what Bishop asked. But I won't fail.

The task will require me to ruin a love—a love I won't be able to heal, mend, fix. I can work stitch by stitch, thread by thread, to put the broken pieces back together, but there will always be one single, broken thread. I can earn forgiveness, but he will never forget. This will become yet another sin that haunts us.

We already have enough sins—enough pain.

So what if I commit one more? Our love has survived before. In some ways, it's survived worse.

No.

Nothing is worse.

"Baby? You okay?" Zeke's voice interrupts my thoughts.

My head is dropped. I never turned the light on, so he can't see my face. I don't want to lie to Zeke, not with my words, but I can let him feel what he wants to feel—reassurance that I'm okay. I just got up to get some water. I'm good. We're good.

Inside my body is in turmoil; my mind is racing to come up with a plan, any plan, that ends with the truth instead of a sin.

I walk over to Zeke and place my hands against his hard, rough chest. I feel my way through his scars, finding his beating heart—so steady, so calm. He's my rock, my anchor. My calm in the storm. Just feeling him now is enough to save me from my future sins.

I stand on my tiptoes, find his lips between his stubble, and kiss him. It's meant to be a reassuring kiss, one to let him know I'm fine. One to let him taste me and realize I haven't spent time getting sick or thinking about Bishop.

But of course, when our lips touch, our fire sparks between us—that need we have and haven't been able to satisfy zips back and forth. I get the pull in my core, tingling between my legs, the need that only he can satisfy. I grab his neck; he grabs my waist, lifts me high, and tilts my head to make it easier to kiss me.

We stumble back, hitting the counter against my ass. I suck his lip. His tongue teases mine. I want to let my hands wander over his body. I want to feel his biceps, his chest, his ass. I want to roll my hips against his body and find the hardness I seek straining against his boxers.

I don't let myself go there. I keep my hands at his neck, letting my hands grip onto his hair for dear life. I'm like a horny teenage boy who wants to fuck his girlfriend for the first time but doesn't want to push her. I don't want to push Zeke. If I do, I could make him feel worse instead of better. There are no guarantees, that's what the doctor said. But I guarantee you that we are going to love each other forever, so we have forever to figure out how to have sex again.

That's what I tell myself anyway when I keep my hands on his neck instead of feeling over his body. Zeke, on the other hand, has no problem letting his hands roam. When his hand finds my breast beneath my shirt, I gasp like it's the first time I've ever been touched.

"These have gotten bigger," he whispers, his stubble brushing against my cheek. I want his stubble against my thigh. It's not fair for him to keep eating me out and not get anything in return. Not fair to either of us. I want a turn to make him feel good, a turn at licking and tormenting and pulling him to the edge of orgasm.

Zeke keeps going, and I know where this is headed—the same thing that has happened every night for the last two weeks. I'll be riding Zeke's face, or he'll have me spread on the bed as three fingers fuck me. I'm not complaining, I could die a happy woman as long as Zeke kept doing that, but tonight, with Bishop in my head, I need more. And Zeke isn't ready to give me what I need yet.

I grab Zeke's hand and pull it away from my chest. Slowly, I let my body fall down from my high as I break our kiss apart.

Zeke tenses but doesn't say anything. He can't push me to let him touch me when I don't get to touch him.

"Is there anything I could do to make you hate me?" I ask, needing to feel connected to Zeke in any way I can. If words are the only way, then so be it. And I need reassurance that if I do what Bishop wants, I won't be ending us. At least not forever.

Zeke turns me around, so I'm facing the mirror, his chest against my back. His hands go around my waist, and his head drops to my ear.

"No. Nothing you could do could ever make me hate you."

"Nothing? That seems impossible."

He shakes his head, his eyes heating into dark, icy slants piercing through the armor I've put up to hide what's really going on in my head. He knows there is a reason I asked my question. He's probing, testing my walls. I won't let him in. This is as far as he gets. I can't break through his armor to be able to touch him, either.

"Nothing—because you love me. Any choice you make, you wouldn't be doing to intentionally hurt me. Your choices would be made in love, even if I couldn't see it."

It's a good answer, but not the truth. He's going to hate me. At least temporarily. He may forgive me, but hating someone you love is easier than he thinks. He's forgotten how I made him feel before when I betrayed him.

I stare at him in the mirror, my eyes threatening him, calling bullshit.

"Is there anything I could do that would make you stop loving me?" I ask.

He draws in a breath like I wounded him simply by asking the question. He finds my left hand in the dark, connecting it to his own. With our hands intertwined, I see our rings touching. Two pieces of metal barely worth a thousand dollars, but to us, they are worth everything.

"Is there anything I could do to make you stop loving me?" his voice is husky as he turns my question on me.

"No, I could never stop loving you."

I feel his heart thumping against my back. It's sputtering at my words, speeding up at my honesty.

His grip on my stomach tightens where my belly has started to protrude, getting thicker but not revealing my secret to the world just yet. He holds my stomach as possessively as he holds the rest of me.

"I will never stop loving you, both of you. I could be

held at gunpoint and told the only way I can live is to stop loving you, and even then, my heart would never betray you. You could murder every other person on the planet, and I would still love you. You could take everything from me, all the money I've ever earned, and I would still love you. You could fuck another man, and I would still love you."

His voice catches, but he forces himself to continue. "You could stop loving me. You could fall for another man, and I would always love you. Our love is different than anything I've felt before. Even Lucy. I loved her, but my love wasn't everlasting. I love my friends, but I would destroy them all tomorrow if it was the only way to keep you. Our love has the power to annihilate entire cities. I would light a city and watch it burn for you."

"I would never ask you..." I say, but I stop myself. We both know it's a lie. I might. I might ask Zeke to do unthinkable things. We have a lot of enemies. I'm sure they all haven't come out of hiding. We will always have enemies. One wrong move means those enemies have power until we destroy them. Those enemies could force us to do horrible, villainous things. We would both do them in a heartbeat to save the other, and to protect our family.

Zeke kisses my cheek. "Don't worry. I'll eliminate our enemies soon. Our family will be safe. We will get out."

He's never admitted he wants to leave this world before. I can't imagine him not carrying a gun every day. I can't think of anything he would enjoy doing more than risking his life to save others. But I understand the desire to get out —to feel safe. I just don't know if getting out will ensure that I'm safe.

Zeke and Enzo have been getting together to plan. This time, I won't be allowed to fight. I have another life to worry about. Risking that life might be the one truly unforgivable sin. But, as Zeke said, it's the one thing I would never do.

"We will get Bishop. We'll drag him here and make him fix you before we kill him," Zeke says.

I nod.

"And Julian—"

"You'll kill him before he says a damn word."

He smirks. "I'm done letting Julian Reed talk. He's a dead man."

I let out a breath, considering telling my last truth when it comes to Julian. But if he's dead, it won't matter. Telling the truth won't change anything—one less pain for Zeke.

Zeke pulls me to him, until my ass is pushed against his hardness.

Wait...

He's hard. I feel it.

My needy eyes meet his. *Does this mean?*

"Soon," he whispers his promise. It's the best damn word he's ever said to me. Soon, I can reconnect with my husband. Soon, we will be whole again. Soon, our enemies will be dead.

20

ZEKE

"Too slow," Enzo says as he punches me lightly in the jaw.

I growl, my head popping back as I try again to swing in his direction without getting hit. This time he hits my stomach before I make contact with his eye.

He's been pulling all his punches every time we've sparred; my broken body can't take a full hit just yet without crumpling. I need the exercise and the practice, though. We are running out of time to defeat Julian and capture Bishop, and I'm a long way from where I should be physically.

I go for a kick. I'm more a punch with my fists kind of guy, but maybe I need to change my game. Enzo grabs my knee, pushing me to the floor.

"Fuck," I growl when he has me pinned beneath him. I'm beyond frustrated at my weak body. I can't get any part of me to work properly. Not my brain, my fists, my legs, my cock. I've been married to Siren for almost a month now, and I haven't fucked her. We haven't even tried, I'm too scared. Sure, I've felt things, gotten hard around her, but not enough to try. *What if I fail? What if I can't satisfy her the way I used to? What if I'm not enough?*

Enzo sighs and hands me a water. "Your head isn't in it today."

"I'm just out of shape."

Enzo sits next to me, but I remain lying on the ground like the weakling I am.

"No, it's more than that. You may not be in great shape or be able to throw punches as quickly as you used to, but there is nothing wrong with your head. You should still be able to anticipate my throws. We've been fighting since we were six. You know my moves. You know my weaknesses and how to exploit them. You haven't even attempted to avoid a punch or thrown anything I couldn't anticipate. What's going on?"

"Nothing. Just tired and want this fight to be over."

"Bullshit."

I stare up at the black ceiling of the boxing room. The room only has a single light shining, but most of the time, Enzo prefers to have the light off so he can train in the dark. He has the upper hand in the dark, that's why most of our advances happen at night. He can see what others can't.

I don't have the sixth sense he does, but I've trained with him in the dark long enough to know how to fight in the shadows as well as the light.

"We have a plan to kill Julian. And I have a team doing round the clock reconnaissance on Bishop. We won't fail. You don't even need to fight. I can handle it and you know it. If the fight needs to go down tomorrow, Kai and I can take care of it. So what the hell is going on?"

I shake my head. I'm not talking to Enzo about my limp dick problem and how I don't think I'll be enough for my wife.

"Nothing." I sit up and drink the entire bottle of water. "I'm just over this today."

"Bull-fucking-shit."

My eyes shoot at him. "Stay out of it. It's not your concern."

"Do you want me to get Kai, so she can drag whatever is stuck up your ass out of you? You've changed. You walk around like a zombie most of the time. I know you. You aren't scared of a fight, even with a kid on the way. You always thought you'd die for someone you love, dying to protect your kid doesn't scare you. So what is it?"

I push myself up. "I'm not doing this."

"Fine." Enzo pulls out his phone and dials. "Stingray, Zeke needs you. He's in the boxing ring."

With that, Enzo walks off steaming.

Instead of running off, I sit on the bench and wait for Kai. I don't want Siren to worry, and she will if I don't convince Kai that I'm fine.

I hear Kai's footsteps.

"I'm fine, Stingray. You don't need to worry about me. Your husband is just overreacting as usual."

"I'm not your stingray."

My head pops up, trying to find her eyes in the dark. It takes me a second, but I see her standing on the mat in the far corner.

"Where's Kai?" I ask.

"She thought you and I should talk. But if you'd rather talk to Kai, I can go get her," Siren says.

"No, I don't want to talk to Kai."

"Good." Siren stretches her arms overhead and then goes through some practice swings.

"What are you doing?" I ask, watching her every move in the dark. Like a dance, she warms up. I'm mesmerized, but also angry, because I know what she's trying to do, and I won't do it.

"Warming up."

"For what?"

"To fight."

"We aren't fighting."

"Yes, we are.

"You're pregnant."

"The doctor said I could do any physical activity that I had been previously doing. Well, before I was pregnant I fought, I boxed, I did Krav Magra. This is perfectly safe."

"I'm not fighting you."

She smirks. "You fight me, or prepare to get used like a punching bag."

I frown, but I find myself standing and walking onto the mat. *What am I doing? I'm not going to fight her.* But my hands are up, protecting my face.

She throws a punch, but not holding back at all like Enzo did.

"Siren, stop."

Another jab hits me on the forearm. It's strong, swift. It's going to leave a bruise on my arm, and most likely, her hand.

"Stop," I say, trying to keep my cool. *She's carrying my baby and willing to risk his or her life for what? To convince me I'm strong enough to fight?* Even if she weren't carrying a baby right now, I wouldn't fight her.

"No, fight me."

She kicks this lunima, hitting my hip—too close for comfort to my fucked up groin.

"Siren." I grit my teeth as I say her name, my anger grinding my teeth together until it's painful.

"Come on, Zeke. Throw a punch. You know I'll dodge it."

"No."

"Why not?" She throws another punch, hitting me in the chest.

"Because you're pregnant."

"You don't have to knock me out, just throw a jab in my direction. Something, anything."

"No."

The hits start coming more rapidly now as she dances around me, her footwork excellent like she's actually fighting me in a ring with judges and everything. I've never just watched her skills before. She's practiced a lot. She has incredible technique, perfected over the years. She's more than capable of protecting herself in a fight.

I'm mesmerized by her feet and not watching her hands like I should. She hits me, full out, on the face. I feel myself falling back, and I don't bother cushioning my fall. I just fall until I hit the hard mat.

Siren stares at me, waiting for me to break, to shatter, to feel something she wants me to feel. But I don't have a clue what she's doing, other than pissing me off.

Carefully, she kneels next to me, glaring at me like she's the one who is pissed instead of me.

"You don't get to be angry. You're the one risking our child's life to make some idiotic point," I say.

"No," she snaps, her words harsh and painful. She takes a deep breath, softening. "You are the one hurting our child by not letting me in. I was patient, and I'll continue to be patient. I don't need your cock to be happily married to you, but I do need my husband. I need him to think of himself as whole and not broken. I need him to fight when things get hard, not give up. You're giving up. You're letting them win. I need you to start fighting again. I need you to take what you want. I need you to—"

I grab her, shutting her up with my lips as I pull her to me. Our lips slam together, her mid-sentence and me parted, leaving us kissing in an awkward meeting. Our mouths half open, our teeth crushing, our lungs half-full of oxygen and carbon dioxide. Neither of us prepared for this kiss.

Siren thought she'd have to push me further to get me to break, and I wasn't expecting to break so easily, but our baby pushed me to the edge. I would do anything—ANYTHING—to protect our child.

Although, this kiss isn't just about our baby. It's about me too. I'm tired of waiting. I'm tired of thinking I'm less than, physically broken. It's time to find out. Time to be brave. Time to push the demons out.

Palmer may have had her own issues that led her to raping me, issues I can forgive her for. But I was still raped, violated in a way I never thought I'd be touched. I thought I could stop it, but I couldn't stop it any easier than I could a bullet entering my body.

My cock has gotten hard plenty of times over the last few weeks. That isn't holding me back anymore.

I push my tongue into Siren's mouth on autopilot, splitting her lips, allowing me entrance the way I've done thousands of times. Our tongues meet in a dance, gliding over each other as we do battle. All the normal things happen. Heat spills between us. Her hands roam over my body. Her nipples pebble. Her moans vibrate in her throat.

All the right things happen to me too. Fire shoots to my belly, my body hardens, and I put everything into the kiss. My erection grows against her belly.

But still...I can't...

Siren senses it first. She stops the kiss, resting her thumb on my bottom lip as we both try to calm ourselves down. We both know this isn't going anywhere.

"I don't want to push you. I just want to help you. I want to know that you're fighting for us, for yourself, and that you're being honest with me and telling me what you need. Whatever you need is fine—therapy, time to heal, another doctor's appointment, going slow, facing your demons, forgiving Palmer or killing her. I don't know how to help you, Zeke. You have to let me in. Our child has the right to know his or her father, not just the piece of him that's left."

I rest my head against her forehead. "How did you get through it so quickly? How can you move on so easily? How are you not reliving every moment Julian was inside you?"

She licks her lips. "You. You were in my head. In some way, I'm afraid of what's going to happen later. Maybe someday, it's all going to hit me, and I won't have done enough work. I won't have healed. But you will. Your brain didn't let you cop-out. You have to face what happened to you. Maybe mine won't let me because it knows you need me first, and once you heal, it will be my turn. But for now, you are the one with a broken heart."

"My heart isn't broken," I sigh, closing my eyes to keep the pain in.

"Tell me," she whispers in the dark. When I don't respond, she hands me some boxing gloves.

I put them on wordlessly, still resting my forehead against hers. I hear her reaching for a boxing mitt for me to hit, and she straps them onto her hands.

"Tell me. Let it all out. Give me everything. Lay it all on me. Let me carry some of your burden because I'm strong enough to handle it."

I swing. I can't even tell what I'm swinging at, but somehow, she makes sure I hit the pad she's holding. It makes a soft squishing sound as the two plastics hit and the velcro holding my gloves on stretches.

"Again," she whispers.

I swing again.

Hit.

It feels good. Not like hitting Enzo, this feels different. Cathartic, in a way. It's easier to pretend like Siren's face is Palmer's. It's easier to be vulnerable with Siren.

It's easier to show her my heart is still bleeding from the wound Palmer caused, no matter how much my bruises have lightened and my scars have softened. I've never had to heal from a traumatic experience before. Every other time, I just healed. The torture never went deeper than the surface. Once the stitches came out, I was good to go.

But this time, it's different.

Siren isn't the only one with nightmares.

I don't sleep—I see Palmer's face.

My brain races around the clock, too afraid of where my thoughts will go if I ever stop and let my mind drift in the silence.

I thought I understood darkness. I thought I understood pain. The physical I can handle, but this—this is like flying in the night with no lights. I'm soaring above the tall buildings, weaving through them. I feel alive like never before. I've tapped emotions I didn't know I could feel, but every second of it is a constant fear of crashing into the side of a skyscraper. And when I crash, that's it—I won't survive.

I thought watching Siren get hurt was going to be the worst pain I'd ever feel. I thought I was the protector who just hurt when I couldn't protect others.

But I've never been violated like that. Never felt what it was like to have something taken from Siren and me at the same time. Never knew how being touched in such a twisted way can also wreck you down to your very soul.

Hit.

The impact rattles through my entire body, jostling free the toxins in my body, setting free the ghosts who haunt me.

I feel the ghosts raging. I swing, again and again, trying to get them out. It's a never-ending battle, though, because every time I knock one out, another pops up. The more I swing, the more I hit, the more I let myself feel the physical, the more the internal takes control.

I think about Siren, and that drives me forward. I don't see her anymore through my haze. I just swing and am confident she won't let me hit her. She won't let me hurt our baby. She's right, it's time. My body has healed. I just have to get the dark thoughts out of my mind.

I'm not good enough.

I'm not strong enough.

I should have stopped it.

My cock shouldn't have gotten hard.

I should have fought harder.

I should have pushed her off me.

I shouldn't have come.

I was bigger than her, but I didn't use my strength.

I was smarter than her, but I didn't use my wit.

I wasn't enough.

I was weak.

I gave up.

I let her hurt me.

I gave up power to a woman who wasn't Siren.

I let a woman I didn't love, ruin me.

I let her touch me.

I let her...I let her...it was my fault.

Swing, swing, swing. I let all the horrible thoughts speak.

Every.

Single.

ONE.

The shame takes over, forcing me to sink lower, but there is no going back now. I'm consumed with it.

I should have stopped Palmer.

It didn't matter that I had been tied up without food or water for days.

It didn't matter that my blood had been pumped with drugs, and my brain was foggy.

It didn't matter that three men had beaten me up, spilled my blood, made my muscles throb with the pain of a thousand dragons breathing fire onto my skin all at once.

It. Didn't. Matter.

When I let her touch me, it was just her and me.

Palmer had removed the chains. I could have stopped her. I could have. I should have. But I wasn't enough.

I wasn't strong enough.

I didn't love Siren enough.

Not enough to stop my body from betraying Siren. My cock got hard. Every thrust of her body over me felt good. When her pussy tightened over me, I exploded inside of her.

I felt her wetness. I felt her shudder over me. I let my cock be fucked by her. Palmer used me, and I didn't stop her.

"I didn't stop her.

"I didn't stop her.

"I didn't stop her!"

The last one is a ferocious scream, like a lion letting the

whole savannah know that I'm king. Except I'm not a king. I'm letting the world know I'm weak, a coward, an adulterer.

I fall to my knees more broken than I've ever been. I hate myself. I can't look at myself in the mirror. I'm not worthy of Siren.

"I'm not enough," I whisper into the darkness, letting my embarrassing secret out. This is how I die—the pain and shame and guilt of letting that woman fuck me when the only woman I want to fuck is Siren.

I'm sure I'm crying.

I'm sure I look like a dying man about to take his last breath.

I'm sure I've never looked weaker. I've never looked more like a fool than I do now.

I'm sure Siren has never loved me less than she does now.

I feel the boxing gloves leaving my hands, but I don't feel Siren.

"I am enough," her voice sings to me, much in the same way her voice called to me the night she saved me from the water.

She sings it over and over, her voice carrying us, demanding all the attention, all the oxygen down to the tiny molecules. Her voice demands every being, no matter how microscopic, pay attention to her.

The vibration of her voice is what hits me first, smack in the chest. Pounding, pounding, pounding into me. Just like the punches I took earlier, it hits me, letting loose more demons in my body. But unlike before, her voice sings louder than the ghosts' voices.

Siren continues to sing, her voice alone destroying the evil inside me. The evil I allowed in.

"I am enough. I am powerful. I am worthy. I am a king. I

am a protector. I am selfless. I am enough," her voice changes tune and melody. It changes pitch going higher and higher, trying to pull me from the darkness of hell and into the light of heaven.

I think she's crazy if she thinks this is going to work, but I'm too exhausted to speak, to move. I've fallen—this is as low as I can possibly go. I've sunk to the deepest parts of hell by betraying the woman I love.

I'm a bad guy.

I deserve it.

This was all just payback for all the men I've murdered, all the women I've failed to save. This is where I belong— suffering, forever.

Siren deserves better.

I shouldn't have let her marry me.

"I am enough. More than enough. I am Zeke. But my name could have as easily been Zeus, the father of all the gods. The strongest, the protector, the one who looked over all the others."

No.

She's wrong.

Her lips are close now, but she doesn't touch me. Not on the lips. Not on the hands. I don't feel her anywhere but in my head.

"Open your heart. Let me in," she whispers before continuing her song. "I am enough. I am love. I am loved. This wasn't my fault. This isn't punishment for my sins. Karma doesn't exist. I'm human, and humans make mistakes. But to Siren, I am a god. I'm her anchor. Her reason for living. The thing tethering her to the goodness in men. I'm a good guy. When I should have punished her, I forgave her. When I should have broken her heart, I married her."

Yes.

I'm her anchor.

I'm her good.

I'm her love.

I think for a minute my heart is going to heal; I'm going to mend. Instead, I feel the pressure building to excruciating painful levels.

"I am enough. I'm worthy. And I'm going to keep my promise to love Siren, forever," she sings again.

That does it—my heart bursts. My world shatters. A dam inside me bursts, and I feel free.

I collapse—the weight gone. Tears are everywhere. I feel like I'm bleeding on that damn floor again with Palmer straddling me about to be taken advantage of.

That should scare me, but it doesn't. When I look up at the gorgeous watering eyes staring over me, when I see the love in her eyes and know that she must have spent hours down here with me in the darkness, I know I am truly loved.

Siren isn't going anywhere. I let her see all of my pain, my shame, my guilt. She understands it all and doesn't care. And now, I know my path forward.

Siren's face watches me carefully, afraid she just lost me again. I grab her hips, helping her to straddle me just like Palmer did in that basement. This dark workout room is mimicking that basement perfectly.

"Zeke, what do you need? Tell me how to help you, and I'll do it," the pain in her voice is still there.

I smirk, grabbing her hair and yanking her down until she can see through my eyes to my soul. "I need you to fuck me, ride me like only you can. I need you to fuck me hard, my beautiful Siren. I need you to remind my cock that you are its master, that I only come for you. I need you to punish me for daring to let another woman touch me."

"Zeke, you have nothing to be sorry for. Nothing I need to punish you for."

"I know." And for the first time since it happened, I believe my own words. I'm angry about what happened to me, but it's not my fault. I need loads of therapy and more time talking about it than I want to admit, but right now, I don't feel my demons. They aren't fluttering around in my heart anymore causing havoc. Siren fought them off.

"But I want you to punish me anyway. I want you rough and hard. I want you to demand my cock to kneel down to his queen and worship you. Fuck me, Siren. Milk me. Remind me of what a stupid ass I've been for not fucking you all these weeks."

Siren bites her lip, and if the lights were on, I know I'd see her cheeks reddening, her eyes dilating. Instead, I settle for thrusting up and hearing the little gasp she makes when my hard cock hits between her legs. I hear her audible gasp.

I grin. *That's right, baby.* I'm about to fuck you like I've never fucked you before. So hold on, and prepare for the ride of your life.

21

SIREN

I WANT TO JUMP UP AND DOWN AND SCREAM FOR JOY. I WANT to run around the yacht and wake everyone up, shouting the good news. I also want to collapse into a ball and sleep for days.

I've never been so exhausted, so drained.

I felt like I just did two Ironmans, a triathlon, and then swam the entire length of the Pacific Ocean.

I never realized the depths of Zeke's pain. He made it seem like it was just his physical body that was hurting. He didn't let me see what was going on inside—the turmoil breaking every cell in his body.

But tonight, I saw it.

I felt it with every punch he threw me.

I heard it with every word he spoke into the darkness.

I tried to take it all away with the sound of my voice. I don't know why I sang. I didn't know if it would work, but singing has always been one of my greatest strengths, my secret weapon.

It worked.

I can hear the change in Zeke's voice. Feel the heaviness lift from the vibrations of his body. His aura is clean again. His heart is mine again. I don't have to fight off Palmer.

Finally, I get what I've wanted for weeks.

What I prayed for.

What I thought might never come.

I get Zeke. All of him.

And damn, is it perfect timing, because I've never needed him more.

I rip my shirt from my body and then tug at his, needing to feel our skins mashed together. We are lying on a workout mat that Enzo and Zeke use to fight each other on. It's covered in sweat, a far cry from the beautiful bed we could be fucking in just a floor above us, but our surroundings don't matter.

I'm not letting anything stop me from having Zeke right now.

"Off," I say, no longer able to form words after singing for three hours straight, singing to his soul and hoping it would listen to me. Hoping my voice would remind him what he already knows inside: he is enough. It isn't his fault what happened. He couldn't have stopped her from taking him any more than I could have stopped Julian from taking from me.

Zeke chuckles as I paw at his shirt in the dark. Our eyes both adjusted long ago, but it's still pitch-black in this room, and my eyes are still human eyes—full of fault, lacking the ability to see much beyond the foot in front of me.

I find Zeke's rough abs, still somehow dipping into deep valleys and high peaks rippling over his body even though his workout routine has reduced significantly since he was injured. His abs are now scarred, but his body refuses to become soft. It refuses to be anything but a brick of muscle, ready to defend me always.

I moan when Zeke's hands push my bra up and find my swollen breasts. They grow larger and more sensitive every day, and Zeke has had plenty of practice finding all the new areas that turn me on now. He works my breasts, molding them, pressing every button before pinching my nipples.

I reach around my back and unhook my bra, needing everything off.

I stand up and shove my leggings and panties down. At this point, they barely fit around my growing stomach. I hear Zeke scrambling to removes his own pants.

I stand over him, listening to him breathe. I'm terrified standing here. I don't know what the end result is going to be. *Am I going to trigger him by trying to fuck him? Especially here, in the dark?*

Did I push him too far? Demand he heals before he is ready?

Even if he's healed emotionally, what if his cock isn't ready? What if he can't perform? Is that going to make everything worse? Undo everything we just healed?

"Siren?" Zeke asks, his voice strong.

"Yes," I try to match my voice to Zeke's, but I know my voice faltered. I know he can hear my fear.

"Get your ass over here and ride me. I've never been harder for you. I've never wanted you more. If you weren't already pregnant, I would fill you with so much of my seed you'd end up pregnant, whether it was the right time of the month for you or not."

I chuckle at his words. They give me strength, just like my song gave him.

I don't think anymore. I'm on the floor, my hips over his, my hands pressed against his chest. My hair is caging in Zeke's head as I breathe over him before going in for a kiss. One final kiss getting us both more turned on and giving Zeke one last chance to back out before we venture into the unknown.

I feel like I'm about to take Zeke's virginity, and I want him to be sure, so fucking sure. I don't want to take anything from him. I want to give him his life back. His strength. His love.

Zeke kisses me, slipping his tongue expertly into my mouth just like he's done a thousand times. There is nothing special about this kiss except what I know is about to follow.

And then, I feel pressure as his teeth roll my bottom lip back and forth between them. My wetness grows between my legs, spilling onto his Zeke's deep V, just above his cock I want so badly.

He presses harder with his teeth and then suddenly releases.

"Fuck me," he growls, gripping my hips and pushing me until I can feel his tip at my slit, but he doesn't push me down. He waits for me to move the final inch.

"With pleasure," I roar as I take all of him at once. His cock rips through my body, and I realize instantly I was wrong when I said I didn't need Zeke's cock before. I was wrong thinking I could live on Zeke's fingers alone, his tongue.

I was so fucking wrong.

His hips rock and mine roll over his, meeting his thrust. It's like the entire ocean is pounding down on top of me. This moment is so intense, in the most delicious, satisfying way.

I didn't realize I was still broken. I was still hurting. I wasn't healed yet. I needed this.

"Why the fuck did I wait six weeks to do this?" Zeke howls as he thrusts in again in long, deep strokes.

"Seven weeks. It was fucking seven."

My nails dig into his flesh.

He hisses.

"I'll never let you go more than seven hours again without my cock."

"Is that a promise?"

"Yes."

"Fuck, we should have put that into the vows."

He rocks again, and I feel him everywhere—all the places I need him.

"Good thing we still need to have another wedding in a courthouse, we can say them then," he grits out. I know he's holding his orgasm back, trying to make this moment last forever.

I rock forward and reach behind, grabbing his balls and squeezing, just enough to punish him.

He bucks like he can't decide if he wants to buck me all the way off him, or if he wants to pull me closer.

"I don't think we can put those in the vows before God."

"Why not?" He breathes deep, his voice so fucking strained.

I open my mouth to speak, but I can't think. My voice doesn't work anymore.

"Exactly," he growls.

And then we are coming. *So. Damn. Hard.*

We both scream so loud that if the room wasn't sound-proof, everyone on the ship would be racing down, thinking we're under attack.

In a way, we did do battle. We both died. And we are now reborn.

This was what we needed.

We needed time.

We needed our bodies to mend.

We needed all our vulnerabilities and shame.

And then we needed to fuck each other dirty and sweating on the floor.

"Thank you," Zeke whispers as I lay on his bare chest. My body is aching for food, for water, for sleep, but I'm not going anywhere. I want Zeke. I want more. One round wasn't enough to satisfy what I've been missing for weeks.

"Thank you," I exhale back.

Zeke strokes my hair, and I grip his.

We breathe a peaceful breath in sync. We did it. We survived. Our horrible past is over.

"My little siren..." Julian says in my head.

I freeze.

"Kiss me like you want me," Julian says, and then I feel his hands on me, touching me...

"Baby? You hungry? Your stomach is growling like I haven't fed you in weeks."

"No, I'm okay," I try to shake Zeke off, but Zeke grabs his shirt, and dresses me in it. He slips back into his boxers. Then he's lifting me, taking me to the kitchen, most likely to feed me.

I shiver, but Zeke just laughs, thinking it was my stomach growling again.

"I'm sorry, little one. I should have fed your mother sooner," Zeke chuckles as he sits me down on a barstool in the kitchen while he goes to work pulling food out. No one is in the kitchen. It's dark outside, probably the middle of the night.

No one sees the moment that Zeke was healed, and mine was torn apart. No one sees the pain I've been fighting down all this time finally got free. No one sees, not even Zeke.

And I won't let him.

I am strong. I am enough. I sing the song I sang to Zeke over and over in my head, but when I hear Julian and Bishop's voice in my head again, goosebumps line my arms, and I know I'm not enough.

22

ZEKE

WE ARE ALL SITTING OUT ON THE TOP DECK—ALL SIX OF US. The twins are down for a nap in their room.

There are maps and documents spread all around. Laptops on several laps. Guns in most of our waistbands. Ammunition in the corner. Knives hidden beneath our clothes.

This is our world—weapons and strategy. Most people will never see war, but we go to war every day.

Siren is sitting on the loveseat next to me. She's not staring at any of the documents, maps, or laptops. She's barely spoken so far as we discuss how we are going to take down Julian and Bishop, and ensure Palmer will never come after us.

Siren seems tired, there are circles under her eyes, and she looks paler than usual. It's not surprising since she spent most of yesterday fighting my demons for me. She also spent most of last night puking in the bathroom. I've tried to get some food in her, but her body can only handle a few saltines at a time. Kai reassures me it's normal, but I don't know how she's going to grow another life only eating a few crackers a day.

"You okay?" I ask. *Genius, my words are.*

She looks at me and nods, but she isn't really looking at me. She's looking past me, like I'm a ghost to her.

I frown.

I take her hand. "Are you upset you can't fight?" I ask, hoping saying the word 'can't' will stir her up.

"Can't fight? Really? I'm only two or three months pregnant. No one can even notice yet. I sure as hell can kick everyone's ass here," Siren roars.

Enzo laughs.

Beckett snickers.

Both men think I've messed up, saying the wrong thing to egg my wife on. Really, I just wanted to bring her back to life, so my plan worked.

I lean over, grab her neck to keep her from pulling away, and whisper in her ear so only she can hear me. "There's my Siren. I thought I lost her."

Her eyes gleam, but then she kisses me tenderly on the lips. "You'll never lose me."

I nod. We both turn back to Kai, who is leading this meeting. Enzo may have more physical skills than Kai, but my stingray has become the master at strategy, and the men follow her better than they ever did Enzo.

"Where are we on Bishop? We have all this information on Julian. We know where he lives. We know how many men work for him. We have his bank accounts. We know he has one of our yachts. But Bishop is like a ghost. We don't even know if that's his first or last name. He doesn't just go by Bishop."

"You go by Black," Enzo says.

Kai sighs. "Have we found anything more?"

All heads shake.

"Dammit. I really wish we knew something about the man."

"It doesn't matter what we know," Siren says. She's been mostly silent, but since she's the only one who has met Bishop, she's the one who we should be listening to when it comes to him.

I take her hand and give it a squeeze, telling her to continue.

"Bishop isn't a good man. His soul is dark. His heart is broken. He has nothing to live for. He doesn't believe in love. He doesn't believe in goodness. He's evil. And he won't hesitate to torture you, not in the physical way you are all used to being tortured, but in a psychological way that will stay with you forever. He'll get in your head, shoving a dagger into your brain, and then twist until you bow to him," Siren's voice falls heavy. Her eyes gloss over, and I know Bishop is in her head again. There is nothing I can do to get him out.

She blinks, clearing her head. "When you see Bishop, you kill him. That's what got Zeke and me in trouble with Julian. We hesitated. He offered us something we thought we needed. He struck a deal with us we thought would save us. Instead, it allowed him time to destroy us."

Everyone nods, hanging onto all of her words.

"I need you all to promise me. When you see Bishop, you'll kill him. You won't hesitate. You won't ask questions. You won't try to save him; he can't be saved. Promise me," Siren says.

Everyone nods again.

"No, with your words. Promise me you won't let Bishop's charms win. Promise me you'll shoot and deal with the consequences later," Siren says.

"I promise," Enzo says.

"I promise," Kai says.

"I don't know how to shoot a gun, but I promise if I learn, I'll kill the bastard," Nora says.

"I promise," Beckett says.

And then Siren is looking at me, like my promise holds more weight than all the rest.

"I'll do whatever you want, but don't you need Bishop to fix you first?" I ask so only she can hear.

"Yes, but I'll take care of that soon."

I frown but trust her. I don't have any other choice.

"I promise," I say, the words feeling ominous.

Siren seems satisfied with all our answers and quiets, giving Kai the floor again.

"We need to get the twins far away from here for a while," she says with pain in her voice.

Enzo takes her hand, agreeing. They both look at Beckett, who they seem to trust with their kids more than anyone else here.

"Of course," Beckett answers with as few words exchanged as possible.

"Nora, can you fly them wherever they want to go? Your plane won't be tracked as easily as if they fly commercial," Siren says.

Nora gives Siren a tight smile. Nora knows Siren is just trying to get her away from here and the impending fight. Nora doesn't have the experience fighting like the rest of us do.

"Yes, I'll go with them." Nora looks to Beckett like she's asking permission to tag along, but he doesn't glance her way.

"Where is the box?" I ask Kai. I feel weird not knowing where they are. I was the one who originally hid the box in the Black vault. I was the one Lucy gave the task to. I feel like this is important, like I should know where the box is now. It's the only way I can protect it.

"Hidden," Kai says.

I frown. "Tell me later?"

"No," Kai and Siren say at the same time.

Enzo and I frown at the two strong-willed women in our lives knowing we've already lost, but not stopping us from fighting anyway.

"Why the hell not? We should all know. If one of us dies, the others should know how to protect it," Enzo says, staring at his wife like she's his insubordinate and not his wife and leader.

"It's not safe. The fewer people that know, the better. That way, the information can't be tortured out of any of us. That way, I'm the only one who they can use in that way," Kai says.

"But—" Enzo starts.

Kai gives him a look, and I know she's playing her power card over him. She's the leader of the Black organization. Normally, Enzo and her run the organization together as equals. I've seen them work together well. But every once in a while, when it really matters, Kai uses her power. She won, after all. Today is for her using that power—for her wielding it like it was always meant to be hers.

"I'm the one who should know. Only me. It's not safe. Bishop knows how to play with our minds; if he captures one of us, he could pull the information out. It's too dangerous in the wrong hands. Only I know," Kai says.

Siren exhales a breath and gives a slight nod of agreement to Kai. I don't know why both women feel so strongly about this, but I trust them both. Even though I think this information should be shared, I won't push it.

"So the plan is to gather every last man and woman willing to fight. To call Langston and drag his ass back here from chasing pussy. Then what?" I ask.

"Then I call Julian or Bishop, and tell them where to find us," Siren says.

I grit my teeth, hating the plan, hating that Siren is the one with the closest connection to the two dangerous men. But it's the best plan we have. It gives us control. We get to decide when and where instead of waiting. And neither men can resist the call of a siren.

The meeting adjourns, and we all go our separate ways. All of us have to start preparing for our different tasks. Nora and Beckett to pack to leave. Kai and Enzo to spend every last second with their twins before they leave. And Siren and I to spend every last second together until I convince her to hide somewhere safe.

It's a monumental task, because even though she's pregnant and has our child to worry about, I know she's going to want to be close. She's going to want to do her part to help kill Julian and Bishop and end this war forever.

We get back to our room, and Siren undresses wordlessly, getting ready for bed. She doesn't speak. She doesn't flirt, trying to get me to kiss or fuck her. There will be none of that tonight. The mood is too somber.

I get undressed and brush my teeth silently next to Siren. Me standing in my boxers. Her in her panties and tank top.

We both spit at the same time.

"What's going on in that head of yours?" I ask.

Siren turns on the water, rinses her toothbrush off like she didn't hear me, but I know she did.

"It's time," she says.

I know exactly what she means. It's time to complete

whatever task she promised Bishop in order for him to set her free, to fix her.

I want to ask her what task Bishop asked of her, but it doesn't matter. Whatever task it is, I'll support her. I want her to be free of him, and if this is the only way to do it, then so be it.

"The fight is coming, and when I call Julian and Bishop to tell them to meet us, I need him to tell me how to fix me on the phone. I know you don't want me here when the fighting starts. This is the only way to ensure I can get fixed and that you can kill Bishop without hesitation when the time comes," Siren continues.

"What do you need from me?" I ask, knowing the only reason she's bringing this up instead of just doing the task is because she needs my help. I don't ask her what she's doing, or how much pain she's about to bring into our lives. It doesn't matter. Our marriage and love can survive anything. We've already proven that.

"I need you to take Kai away for a couple of hours. Wait until after the twins are gone," Siren says.

I suck in a breath, knowing I'm about to choose my wife over my friends. Siren has to do something to hurt them.

Her eyes are sad and heavy staring at me. Her eyes hold the weight of everything she is about to do.

I step toward her, resting my hands on her hips by her growing belly, holding our child. My eyes stare her down, showing her everything I'm feeling.

"Whatever you need, I'll do it. It's no longer a choice between you and everyone else. I'll always choose you. You'll always come first. Don't ever hesitate to ask of me. Don't worry that you're making me choose—you aren't. When it comes to you and our baby, it's never a choice. You are first. You will always be first."

Her lips press against mine softly, and for a second, I feel like she's poisoning me with her lips, putting me under her spell, softening me to her, bending me to her will. Her lips are that of a siren's.

She's about to use her powers to hurt someone I care about, but it doesn't matter. I've been in love with her from the start. She didn't have to use her powers on me, I've always been her's.

Tomorrow, I'll realize just how deep her talons have a grip on my heart.

23

SIREN

EVERYONE IS GONE.

Well, everyone I need gone is gone.

Beckett and Nora took the twins far away. I don't know where, and I absolutely don't want to know. I don't even know if Kai and Enzo know where they went. I don't know if Beckett and Nora had a plan when they left, other than to take them far way, to hide them. To keep them secret from Julian and Bishop. I'm sure they already know about the twin's existence.

Both men are devils, but I don't think even they would stoop to involving the kids unless they had no other choice to get what they want.

Kai left with Zeke this morning, to make the rounds to all the yachts and prepare them for the upcoming battle. It took zero persuasion from Zeke to convince Kai to go with him. No explanations were needed to convince Enzo as to why the two of them should be the ones to go instead of Enzo and Kai.

Everything has been set up for me to do what I need to do, but instead of getting to work right away, my stomach has been more upset than usual, like my body knows how much this is going to hurt me. How this is going to hurt everyone. Relationships are going to change after this. I'm about to do something unforgivable, something I don't ever want to ask forgiveness for, but something I have to do for my unborn child. My child deserves to have a mother who isn't controlled by a mad man. I can't risk that Bishop could put thoughts in my head that could tell me to hurt my own child. I won't let that happen. I won't.

That's what I think about as I kneel on the tile floor of the bathroom hunched over the toilet. My stomach is twisted, my mouth burns with the taste of my vomit, and my head is sweaty—the complete opposite of what I need to feel and look in order to complete my task.

"Zeke, please forgive me," I say before I push myself off the floor.

I should have already started my plan, but even now, I continue to put it off. I decide to shower first. I spend at least a half an hour scrubbing every inch of my skin, arguing it's important to get all of the vomit smell off, not because I'm stalling.

Then I take another twenty minutes blow-drying my hair.

Another fifteen painting my face with blush and red lipstick.

I waste another thirty minutes finding just the right outfit, even though I end up picking the outfit I started with —a tight-fitting red dress that my black lace bra peeks out the top and that can easily be hiked up. I strap my gun around my thigh, just in case.

Finally, I stare at myself in the mirror—this time the act has nothing to do with me stalling.

This is the last time I'll be able to look at myself and not truly see the siren inside me. It was one thing to use Zeke. I did it out of love for him, and it turned out for the better in the end.

This.

This isn't like that.

This is cementing my place in hell.

I know I chose my outfit correctly from my sharp heels, my skin-tight dress, the color of my lipstick. My hair is stick straight, and when I run my hand through it and flip it so the part is no longer perfectly in the middle but off to one side, I'm a she-devil ready to pounce.

"You're a siren. Aria is gone. You claimed to enjoy being a siren. This is what comes with it. I have to take the good and the bad. My skills can be used against me."

I push all of that out.

Time to go to work.

I step out of my bedroom with confidence. I have a plan to complete Bishop's task, and I know it will work, but it will destroy two unbreakable bonds in the process.

No bonds are unbreakable, Bishop says. *Everyone can be broken.*

I disagree, but I know in my heart he's right. I'm about to prove his point.

I walk up the stairs to the top of the yacht. I had one of the guards bring up the small keyboard piano that I found in one of the twin's playrooms. I sit down at the keys. I stop thinking, and I just play.

I play every tormented love song I can think of, every painful story.

Then I cast the final hook—I sing.

My voice carries throughout the entire ship—calling to the man I seek. I hope the servants are smart enough not to listen to my call, because I just need one man, and I need him alone.

I hear footsteps, but I don't stop. I can't stop. Once I'm in a trance like this, I'm just as much at the mercy of it as the people listening. I keep playing. I keep singing until the last note of the song is over.

"Beautiful," my mark says. I don't turn around. He could have chosen a different word to describe what he heard. He could have said amazing, incredible, wow. Instead, he chose the word I knew he would. He can't help himself. He doesn't realize the importance of words.

Only someone like me who has been careful with words all her life, careful not to tell a lie, would understand the importance of word choice.

I let my hands dance across the keys, but I don't speak. I need him to move closer. I need to pull him in—a word isn't enough.

He clears his throat. "You look beautiful. Waiting for Zeke?"

I turn my head, giving him a partial view of my face, knowing it will draw him in further. Not because he's a man near an attractive woman, but because he's polite and will want to look me in the eyes when he speaks to me.

"Yes. We've never had a date. I thought having one under the stars before we were separated sounded like a good idea. Is it foolish of me to think they will be back soon?" I ask.

Enzo chuckles and moves closer, until he's sitting down on the piano bench next to me. "Yes, those two will be gone for a while still. There are a lot of ships they need to visit."

"And they love each other," I finish.

He sighs, and that's when I notice he has two wine glasses filled with red wine.

"That for me?"

He shrugs. "I know some women still drink a glass of wine, even while pregnant. I thought it was wrong for me to drink and at least not offer you some."

Such a gentleman. And I'm going to play to all his gentlemanly weaknesses.

I take the wine glass and take a sip. Drinking wine is the least risky thing I'm going to do when it comes to risking this baby's life.

Enzo does the same, his heavy eyes looking at me.

"It doesn't make you nervous that your stingray is with my anchor?" I ask, using both Kai and Zeke's nicknames.

"No." Enzo takes a drink of his wine, but his eyes tell me he's lying. They wrinkle in the corners as the truth pulls at him.

"What are you afraid will happen?" I ask, trying again. Drinking my wine so Enzo will drink his. I don't want him drunk; I don't like using drugs to manipulate the men I target. It doesn't seem fair. But I want him relaxed, willing to do things he might otherwise not do.

"The same thing you're afraid will happen."

I laugh like he's ridiculous, even though we both know how easy it is to fall over the line from friends to lovers. From enemies to everything.

I take another sip of wine, then set it on the edge of the piano. My hands are lightly stroking the keys again as I play a soft melody.

"I'm not afraid of anything."

Enzo chuckles deeply. "Now, who's lying?"

"I'm not lying. They could sleep together, and it wouldn't hurt me."

"That's not what I'm afraid they are going to do. You really think Kai and Zeke would sleep together?"

Yes, fall into my trap. Fall so this can be over.

"Don't you?"

"No. I don't."

"Then what do you think?"

I continue to play, knowing this closeness is enough to draw Enzo in. I don't need the sexy clothes. I don't need the wine. I don't need my sultry voice. I need him talking. I need him thinking about Kai. I need him longing for something he thinks he's yet to find.

Humans are simple creatures. We aren't complicated. We all yearn for the same thing—to feel the greatest love.

Enzo and Kai have a relationship that I could only dream of sharing with Zeke. They have a trust in each other that I don't know if Zeke and I can truly have considering our past and how we started.

Yet somehow, Enzo still thinks there is more to be had. He sees the way Zeke calls Kai 'Stingray,' and he thinks he's missing out on some part of his wife. He thinks Kai shares something with Zeke she will never share with him.

She does.

But it's different. It's not Enzo's; it's Zeke's. Enzo and Kai are soulmates, but so are Zeke and Kai. They were all destined to be in each other's lives. All destined to love each other, in the exact way they've come together. There is no Enzo and Kai without Kai and Zeke. No Kai and Zeke without Enzo and Kai.

But the heart can be easily made jealous. Enzo is weak right now. He's worried about his wife, his kids. Scared to death that because he chose this life, a life that involves many enemies, that that means he doesn't deserve his family.

I know because I feel the same way.

For a while, I just play as the dark sky spreads over us. I

don't know when Zeke and Kai will be back; I just know my plan will work. It has to for my own kid's future.

"Did Kai tell you where the box is?" I ask, raising my eyebrow at him.

He freezes, his wine glass hovering in front of his mouth.

"I'm not asking because I want to know where they're hidden. I don't." *Please, don't tell me. I don't want to know. Please let Kai have been smart enough not to tell him.* I'll find out if she did, and I can't know. "I'm just curious if she told her husband."

Enzo lowers his wine glass. "She didn't tell me."

He puts the glass down on the other end of the piano. Then, to my surprise, his fingers start playing.

"You play?" I ask, even though it's obvious he does.

"No, but I'm a fast learner."

His hands mimic mine, just an octave lower.

"That's incredible. I was always a slow learner."

"Really?" he asks, surprised.

"Yep, until my twenties. Then all of a sudden, everything I'd studied for years clicked. I learned how to become a fast learner."

He moves his hands differently on the keys, and I copy.

He smiles.

We continue to move our hands over the keys until I can't help but sing the melody in my soul. One of longing to be with the one you love. One I know will speak to Enzo's soul.

Eventually, he stops moving his hands over the keys. He just watches me. With how passionately I'm playing, my dress has hiked up high on my thigh, my straps have fallen off my shoulders, and my cleavage is spilling out of the too-tight dress.

I study Enzo out of the corner of my eye. His sleeves are rolled up, and the top few buttons of his shirt are undone. He's almost as dressed up as I am. It's clear he had the same thought that I'm pretending to have, to dress up for one last romantic moment with the one we love. Instead, we are sharing it together.

"Do you think we share the same kind of connection Kai and Zeke share?" Enzo asks.

No.

Hell no.

But this is the moment I've been waiting for. Enzo isn't drunk, but he's lost. He doesn't hear the voices downstairs. He doesn't know the trap I sprung.

"Maybe. But what is that connection they share exactly?"

I turn sideways on the bench, putting one leg on either side, so I'm straddling it, pushing my dress so high up on my thighs he can see my underwear.

"A deep friendship?"

My eyes seer. *You can do better, Enzo.*

"Really? They are just really good friends? Oh, Enzo, are you really that naive?"

"They aren't lovers!"

"I never said they were."

"You implied it." His face is red. He's angry. He goes to stand up, but I grab his shirt, yanking him down and also to me.

I can do this. We are so close. So fucking close.

"No, but you did. You think they could be. They might, in a moment of weakness, give in to their temptation. Maybe not tonight, but in the past."

He frowns.

"Maybe it's not the past you are worried about but the

future. What happens if you and I die? Will they comfort each other through their mourning?"

I curl my hand around his neck.

His brow jumps in shock.

Then he realizes what I'm doing—showing him it could never be true because when I touch the nape of his neck, he feels nothing. How wrong he is...

"Will they accidentally kiss each other in a drunken night, much like this?"

I swing my leg over his lap, my time running out as the footsteps grow louder. His eyes darken in a warning.

"Will they fuck and realize they should have been doing it this entire time? Realize we were never the people they were in love with, it was always each other?"

He shudders, disturbed. I lean toward him. Our lips almost brush.

"If we died, I would want them to find each other. I would want them to be happy. They deserve to be happy if we are gone," he says.

"What if they would be happier with each other now?"

"They wouldn't."

"What if we would be happier?"

"We wouldn't."

"Prove it. You know you need to."

"I don't need to prove anything," Enzo says.

Such a gentleman. I hate doing this, but I don't have a choice. It's now or never.

I grab his hands and place one on my ass, the other on my breast.

"Feel anything?"

"No."

"What about now?" I ask as I kiss his neck.

He stiffens.

"Siren," his voice warns, hating my fire on his neck as much as I hate my tongue licking over his neck.

He tries to push me off him, but he won't dare hurt me since I'm pregnant. So I take what I need from him. I become all the people I hate—Palmer, Julian, Bishop. I take from Enzo, knowing he's defenseless.

I undo his pants and slip inside, avoiding his cock, but accidentally brushing against him all the same. It's not about me violating him; it's about what it looks like to Zeke and Kai.

"You're a liar, Enzo. You want me," I whisper.

"No. Siren, stop."

Forgive me. Please, fucking forgive me.

I see Zeke's eyes. I see them burn into me.

"Want me to stop?" I whisper into Enzo's ear so that Zeke and Kai can't hear the words I speak, but they will hear Enzo's reaction.

"Yes!" he screams. His voice screams everything he wants. He wants me to stop, but to them, it looks like he's begging me to touch him.

My eyes go to Zeke—*I always tell the truth, even when I lie. Find the lie, Zeke. Find the truth. You know this isn't what I want.*

I take the last thing I require of Enzo Black, the great man who can so easily be taken down against his will by a woman. I won't rape him. That was never the goal, but I take everything from him all the same.

He will be able to get it back, eventually. He will be able to remind Kai that he loves her, that I was the monster tonight, not him. But for now, his life will be broken—as was required of me.

I take the final thing, destroying myself more than I destroy him. I didn't rape Enzo like Julian did me. I won't milk Enzo dry like Palmer did to Zeke. But I fucked with Enzo's head like Bishop did me. And I touched him where I had no right to.

I'm a monster.

A devil.

There is no forgiveness to be had. I won't ask for it either. I keep the tears in. I don't get to be in pain as I do this, as I take everything from the three people on this deck.

I tilt my head, flash Zeke a lustful look so not even he can tell the truth from the lies, and then I kiss Enzo open-mouthed. I kiss him with every emotion I have. I do what Bishop commanded—I kiss Enzo. I destroy two marriages, and I pray like hell we will all survive this.

I didn't understand why Bishop wanted me to do this before, but hearing the collective gasp of the room, feeling the shift in the air, his motive is clear. Bishop wanted us all weak when he fought us. He knew together we could never be beaten, but apart, we are easy targets.

I did this. I destroyed our chance at killing our enemies so I could get Bishop out of my head. I just hope it's worth it.

24

ZEKE

SIREN KISSED ENZO.

Yes, my brain is going to be processing what I saw for a long time.

No, it wasn't a dream.

Yes, it was real.

Why? I have no fucking clue what this could have to do with a task Bishop gave her.

My body floods with rage, with anger, with undeniable and uncontrollable pain. I realize this might be my most desperate moment.

Not learning that Siren scammed me.

Not finding out that she was married to another man.

Not having her ripped from me and raped by a man she works for.

No—this guts me worse than all of those. Not because a kiss is somehow worse. Not because the compromising position they were in is too horrible for my eyes to bear. But because of the vows we made, the promises, they mean nothing if we don't keep them. We aren't legally married. The only way we stay married is if we both want to be married. We both dream this dream and want each other more than we want to be apart.

And in one moment of weakness? Of lust? Enzo and Siren threw away everything. Because what? We were fucking gone too long?

Siren told me to take Kai away, so I did. I took her away all damn day. I gave Siren as much time as she could possibly want to complete her mission. I assumed her mission was finding out the location of the box to turn over to Bishop.

I assume that's still what she was doing when she was kissing and dry humping my best friend. She's used to seducing men to get the information she needs, but I'm angry she couldn't come up with any other way to get him to spill.

I can think of a hundred different ways, none of them involve almost fucking my best friend.

The cool air has turned hot, suffocatingly hot, even though we are standing on top of the yacht with plenty of air to be shared between the four of us.

We've paired off in a staring contest of two versus two. I'm staring at Siren. Kai is staring at Enzo. We don't acknowledge the other people up here with us.

My heart doesn't break watching Siren still sitting on Enzo's lap, caressing his head, hiding behind him, using him like a shield to protect herself from me.

I growl, my face turning into a dark shadow. Siren doesn't get to hide. She doesn't get to pretend she was telling the truth while all the time, showing the world a lie. This time, I'm going to make her face the music. She's going to have to own the consequences of her actions.

I put my hands into my leather jacket pockets, though. I

can be patient when I want to be. I can wait to get her alone before we talk. So I stand silently.

I'm not going to help her out of this uncomfortable situation. Siren didn't want to talk to me ahead of time and tell me her plan. She doesn't trust me to help her, so I don't trust her with my truth, with my current feelings. She could have told me her plan, and I could have told her she's a damn fool. Then we wouldn't be in this situation.

Kai, on the other hand, doesn't have any patience when it comes to making her vengeance known. All of it is directed at her husband.

"How dare you! After everything we've been through, you do this!" Kai screams, marching over to her husband.

Enzo jumps, so does Siren. Siren is off Enzo's lap as Kai marches over, but her hand gets stuck in his zipper. Siren shoots me a 'help me' glare.

No. Fucking. Way.

You got yourself into this mess, pretty girl, you can get yourself out.

Finally, Enzo yanks her hand free, and Siren stumbles away from Kai just before she slaps Enzo hard across the cheek. He takes it, as he should.

"How could you?" Kai's voice is eerily calm after just being wild.

Enzo stiffens but doesn't speak. There are no apologies or excuses he could give that would make this moment better.

"Are you drunk?" Kai asks, sniffing his breath.

"No," Enzo says. It's clear he isn't drunk. And if he was, he would definitely be sober now. His clothes don't look good, though. His shirt is unbuttoned halfway down. His pants are undone with the top of his pubic hair protruding.

I don't dare look at Siren. I focus on the disaster in front of me. I don't want to see her dress out of place. I don't want to see it ripped or undone. I don't want to see her nipples hard or her panties wet. I don't want to see her flushed cheeks or swollen lips. I don't want to see any evidence that another man touched my woman.

"Did the whore drug you?" Kai hisses, staring from Enzo to Siren.

I growl, "Too far." Apparently, I'll still protect Siren even when I shouldn't.

Kai flips me off, returning her glare to her husband, begging him to give her a reason for this situation. One where he isn't at fault, but he's as much at fault as Siren is. He could have stopped her at any time. He didn't.

"No," Enzo says, sealing his fate.

I don't understand what happened. I know that Siren can seduce. I know her voice is heavenly—it's what healed me. But I don't understand how two married people could end up kissing, with hands in places they shouldn't be. *If we hadn't walked in, then what would have happened? How far would they have gone?*

Kai slaps Enzo again.

"Stingray," he says, his voice begging to let him talk.

"Don't!" Kai takes a shuddering breath. "Don't. You don't get to call me that. Not anymore. Only Zeke can call me that."

I gulp, not liking that at all. With as pissed as Kai is, I wouldn't doubt if she wanted to kiss me right now to get back at Enzo. She stomps over to Siren, and I instinctively go over. I'm pissed at Siren, but I won't let Kai touch her.

"How could you?" Kai says, her heart breaking.

It's then I realize my heart isn't broken. It's just hardened, putting up shield after shield, not wanting to allow Siren back in again. But there's a problem—Siren is already on the inside with me. I should have pushed her out before I started putting my walls back up.

Kai moves her hand up to slap Siren, so I move to prevent her from touching Siren, but Kai's hand falls on my cheek.

I blink rapidly, not understanding.

"I can't slap Siren because she's pregnant," Kai says, like that somehow makes sense for her to instead slap me.

Kai turns in her boots and marches down the stairs. Enzo takes a deep breath like he's gaining courage. He doesn't look at me or Siren. He's focused on his wife. Then he's gone too.

It's just me and Siren alone on the top deck, with nothing but the stars and the sound of the waves.

"I'm—" Siren starts.

"If you end that sentence with 'sorry,' I'm going to jump over the railing and swim until I'm too exhausted to swim anymore. Until I drown in the ocean like I should have all those months ago. I don't want to hear your excuses. I don't want to know why. I don't want some inexcusable apology. Just..." I throw my hands up, but I have no idea how to make this better. No idea what to say or do. "Just..." I try again. But again, I don't know what I need.

My eyes look at Siren, really look at her for the first time. I see her disheveled hair where Enzo's hands touched. I see her smeared lipstick and raccoon eyes from her running mascara. The straps of her dress are halfway down her biceps. Her black lace bra is completely visible on one side. Her dress is still pulled up high on her thigh.

I grind my teeth, my jaw clenching, my veins bulging. I ball up my fists. I need to punch something. I should find Enzo and beat the shit out of him. I don't understand what happened exactly. They both were dressed up. *Why?*

"Did you complete your task?" I ask, carefully and slowly. I need to know this was all for something. That Siren gained some freedom when she kissed Enzo. I need to know this wasn't all for nothing.

She nods.

I can't look at her. I stare out at the dark ocean, but I can still see her out of the corner of my eye. She doesn't look ashamed. She doesn't look scared. She doesn't look angry, timid, or lost. She looks begging. Not for forgiveness, but for something else I don't understand. I thought I knew all of her looks, but this one I've yet to learn. Right now isn't the time for me to study this new one.

"Good," I finally say, and then I'm walking away. I think she might follow me, but as I descend the stairs, I'm alone. I don't hear her footsteps. I don't feel her presence.

I go all the way to the deepest part of the ship into one of the rooms Enzo and I use to monitor security systems. I unlock the door and step inside. Siren doesn't have the access code to my knowledge. She can't get in if she comes looking for me.

I slam the door, but it doesn't make me feel any better.

"Siren, what have you done?" I fall into the spinning chair and kick my feet up onto the desk.

I listen at the door. She's not coming after me. I would feel her descending already even before I heard her.

Siren would have felt the same. That's how connected we are. When she kissed Enzo, she would have felt us coming. Definitely heard our footsteps and voices. I know she saw me before she kissed him. *But how many kisses did they share before we arrived? Was that the only one?*

Siren knew we were there, and she kissed him like that was the reason for kissing him.

"Stop thinking about it, asshole," I murmur to myself. I

need some time to calm down, but I don't know how to do that.

I see a bottle of bourbon sitting on the desk. I grab it and hold it to my chest like I'm going to get the effects of the alcohol simply by pressing the bottle to my body. I pick up my phone and press the number without thinking it through.

Langston, one of my other best friends, is supposedly off chasing down his girlfriend, Liesel. But right now, I need him. I don't give a damn that he hasn't answered any of my other phone calls. I need him, so he better fucking answer.

His voicemail greets me instead, but I still need to talk.

"Langston, you asshole, this is Zeke. Your best friend you left for dead. Yea, I'm alive, you motherfucker. I'm alive, and you haven't come to see me. What the hell is that? I know you are trying to win Liesel back, but I came back from the dead—I think that warrants a visit from my best friend.

"Yea, that's right. I called you my best friend. And right now, I mean it, even though you're on my shit list for not coming to see me already. You have no idea the shit I'm in. Stingray is broken. I can't be there for her this time, because her fucking husband kissed my wife! Yep, you heard me correctly. I have a wife. I'd love for you to meet her, even though I'm pissed."

I stare down at the bottle I want to completely consume. I'm sure the answering machine has cut me off by now, but I keep talking anyway.

"I'm lost, man. I've never felt this lost and scared before. I didn't know what love could do to a man. Now I know. Loving someone makes me crazy. It fucks with my head. It makes me weak and vulnerable. It makes it so she's the only person in the world I care about liking me. I don't even care if I fix my relationship with Enzo, I just want to fix things with her.

"And no, it's not just so I can get some pussy, although having the same magnificent woman to come home to every night is nice. No, I just want...fuck, just come back, man. I don't understand what your deal is, but a fight of epic proportions is about to go down. I need you. We all do. Just get your ass back here and bring Liesel. I know me and her don't always get along, but if you love her, then that's enough for me. I'll go to battle for you to keep her. But I need my best friend by my side, and that's you, asshole. Just don't tell Enzo that. Or Kai. Or Siren."

I end the call and toss my phone on the counter. I should drink the entire bottle of whiskey in my hand and then sleep the rest of the night in here. But after everything we've been through, all the danger we've experienced, I know life is short. There are no guarantees that we get tomorrow. I've waisted too much time not spent with Siren. I'm not going to waist another second.

I set the bottle down and then make my way back upstairs, Siren still waiting. She's sitting at the piano; her fingers curled over the keyboard. She's not really playing; she seems more angry with the piano than anything. She bangs on it roughly, then apologizes sweetly as she moves her fingers over the keys.

And then, she stops. Her fingers are no longer gliding. She's reaching for a wine glass next to her, her head is turned, and I see the mascara lines down her cheeks where her tears have fallen.

She takes a large gulp of the wine, thoroughly pissing me off.

"You shouldn't be doing that," I growl. I guess it's time to show her how angry I am.

25

SIREN

Zeke came back. *Did he figure out the truth?*

Or is he here to punish me for hurting him? For destroying two relationships with one kiss? For proving that no relationship, no matter how loving, is unbreakable?

"Put the wine glass down," he growls. He's pissed I'm drinking while pregnant.

"No. I'm sure you're drunk off your ass. I think I can have one glass of wine," I spit back. I don't even know why I'm drinking the wine at all. I don't want to hurt my baby in any way, but I'm so damn afraid. I know I'm fucking this all up. I don't know how to help. I don't know how to keep my baby safe. I can't even keep myself safe.

"I'm not drunk." Zeke walks toward me, but I don't give him my full attention. I'm still seated at the piano, gripping my wine glass like a shield.

"Sure, you aren't." I roll my eyes, lifting the glass to my lips again, needing to feel something, but I can't. I don't even feel sorry about what I did. It had to be done. If I really love Zeke and he really loves me, then our relationship will survive. And this is barely a blip on Kai and Enzo's relationship. They will be made up by the morning if they aren't already.

Zeke stands over me, breathing down on me. I don't smell a drop of alcohol on his breath.

"I'm not the one who is lying," Zeke says, yanking the glass from my hand and throwing it on the floor, shattering the crystal glass into thousands of pieces.

He knows. He knows why I kissed Enzo. Why I shoved my hand in his pants and made us look like we had been making out for hours instead of just the single kiss.

"Can we fix this?" Zeke asks, his eyes searing down at my flesh, my overexposed skin in this dress.

I swallow hard against the growing dryness of my throat caused by Zeke's intense stare. "We could, but we shouldn't —yet."

"Did you call Bishop?"

"Yes. I'll be fixed tomorrow morning," I say, also indicating when Bishop will attack us. Bishop won't wait, not now that our world is in chaos.

Zeke stares up at the sky like he wants to curse the stars for letting this happen, for the pain he's feeling. He has no idea how hard it was to betray him like that, knowing it was the only way to protect him. He doesn't know what I know. He doesn't know the truth. And hopefully, I will have fixed everything before I have to tell him, before he knows the thoughts in my head.

"I should hate you," Zeke says calmly.

"You should," I agree.

"But I don't."

I nod, already knowing that. It's why Bishop's plan is stupid. His plan will only work for a few hours. The chaos and turmoil we feel will last less than twenty-four hours. Our relationships are too strong.

Zeke stares at the piano like it's his enemy. "Play for me."

"Why?"

"Because you owe me." His eyebrow raises in a snarky way.

He's right. I do owe him.

But I want to burn the piano to the ground, destroying the evidence of my sin. I don't want to play.

Zeke takes a seat on the bench facing the piano, spreads his legs wide, and then pats a spot on the bench in between his legs and the piano.

I move to sit down next to him instead of in front of him, but Zeke grabs my hand and pushes me into the small space in front of him. The back of my dress is mostly backless, so my skin is flush against his front. I can feel the coolness of his leather jacket, combined with his warm breath, on my bare skin.

"Play for me," he breathes. "Not like you played for him. I want a song all my own."

Chills dance over my skin at his words. I bite my lip, trying to keep the feelings at bay. He's not going to let me act on my feelings. He may be forgiving, but he's not going to fuck me after seeing my tongue down one of his best friend's throats.

I rest my hand over the keys, considering what song I want to play.

"Don't get stage fright now. Play for me," Zeke growls impatiently in my ear, taunting me, telling me he knows it wasn't this hard for me to sing for Enzo, so it shouldn't be hard to play for him either.

But it is. Playing for Enzo was about manipulating him. Playing for Zeke is about showing him that I love him more than life itself. That every sin I commit, every truth I tell, is for him.

My hands fall to my lap as I can't come up with a song to play. Zeke puts his hands on top of mine and brings them to the piano. "Play, Siren. Just play," his voice is kinder now, with plenty of begging. He needs this.

I don't think. I play. At first, my fingers just move over the keys in a familiar way, combining several popular songs. I play a little of Bieber, Swift, and Eilish. But quickly, my fingers take on a life of their own. I no longer recognize the melody I'm playing, but it's a beautiful, haunting sound. One that drives me to play faster, to find the next verse, the next melody. I become greedy, wanting to hear the song I've just created. I want to know. I want to hear it.

More. More. More.

I chase the keys, letting the emotions of the song drive through me until I'm consumed by them.

Zeke's hands run up and down my arms, feeling me play in a new intimacy. His head rests on my shoulder. His legs wrap tighter around my hips until it feels like we are both playing together.

"Sing," Zeke says, his throat dry as he speaks the word like a command and a desire.

I open my mouth, having no clue what's going to come out. At first, it's a hum, a single syllable. But then the words come to me, like a gift from the gods.

I step off the cliff and then I'm falling.
The jump is freeing.
I could be flying.
Drifting higher and higher.
A bird in the sky.
I feel so light; I'm sure the air could lift me up.
But I'm not flying.
I'm falling.
Falling through time and space.

Falling through your open hands.
Falling to the deepest hell.
I won't survive the fall.
I don't need to either.
Don't catch me.
Promise, to never catch me.
Just don't let our love fall.

My song is a cry to Zeke to trust me. To love me. To never hurt me. To never betray our love. It's a promise that I will never betray him either, even when it appears like I am.

Zeke lifts my hands from the piano, and my song stops.

"I hate what you did," Zeke says honestly.

"I do too."

"I won't ask you why."

I nod.

"I want to fuck you," he whispers into my ear.

I bite my lip. "Bishop is watching. He has eyes on one of the other yachts."

Bishop told me he had men watching us. Men whose loyalty was to him, not Kai and Enzo.

Zeke stiffens, his eyes searching out in the darkness like he could see the betrayer through the blackness and miles between us.

"Take from me," I say, knowing we still need to appear angry with each other so Bishop will think I did a good job.

Zeke frowns.

"You want me. You take me," I say, needing this so badly. I need him to be rough. I need him to claim me as his.

"You sure?" his voice so damn low and raspy.

"More than I want my heart to keep pumping my body with blood."

His eyes tell me all I need to know. That this is an 'I love you' fuck, not an 'I hate you' fuck, but from the outsider's view, no one would know.

Except us—we will know. This is all about our complicated love story.

Zeke's hands dance one by one down my bare back. I tense with each touch, trying to keep the ecstasy off my face. Zeke has the power to fucking demolish me with one kiss. One kiss could change everything. *If he had kissed Kai and I'd walked in, how would I feel?*

Devastated.

Despondent.

So lost and broken.

The fact that Zeke can sit here and hold me right now, that he wants to kiss and fuck me, just shows that he is the better person. He's so much better than I am. So much better.

His hand continues down until he touches the zipper of my dress. I think he's going to unzip it, reveal more of my skin, but he doesn't.

I lick my lips and lean back toward him, begging for a kiss. I would beg on my knees if it meant he would kiss me.

Instead, Zeke's eyes darken as he grabs my chin. "You think I want to kiss your mouth after you kissed him?" He chuckles darkly. Then his hand goes up my back, until he's fisting my hair, pulling my head back roughly, exposing my neck and chest to him.

His teeth bite on my clavicle like he's a goddamn vampire. Apparently, I'm into vampires because my insides flood with desire and an ache only Zeke can cause.

"Did Enzo turn you on like this?" Zeke asks roughly, even though he already knows the answer.

"No."

Zeke kisses up my neck, and his hand pushes into my

bra, finding my nipple and pinching it harshly. "Did he touch you like this?"

"No," I gasp, feeling too good. My head falls back on Zeke's chest. There is no way Bishop's spies wouldn't think I'm enjoying every second of this. But Zeke's dark eyes, gruff voice, and anger might save us. There is no denying his pain etched into every hard line of his face.

Suddenly, Zeke jerks us up off the bench and bends me over the piano. My hands bang against the keys as I hold on. Zeke is bent over me. His hands are gliding down my body, claiming every part of me. "Did you fuck him?"

"No."

Zeke pushes my dress up over my ass, and then he's yanking my panties down, his finger finding how wet I am as he dips slowly inside me, teasing me but not giving me what I want.

"Did you get wet for him?"

"No, only you."

"Damn right. You are mine."

He slaps my ass hard. This isn't for show. This is because he's angry.

I hear his zipper, but Zeke is still clothed. He's going to fuck me with his clothes on. He's going to fuck me without letting me touch him.

"Zeke, I need—" I try to reach back, but he grabs my wrists. He yanks them behind my back, pulling roughly until my shoulders ache at the tension.

And then his cock is pushing at me. But he's not pushing at my entrance. He's pushing at my ass.

"Zeke," I warn. I'm terrified Julian is going to end up back in my head again, all my trauma flooding back. I want to be here with Zeke, not trapped in my nightmares.

He keeps my hands pulled back. My legs are spread for

him, and my ass is his for the taking. I feel his cock so hard at my back entrance.

He puts his hand in front of my lips. "Spit."

I do, watching his eyes eat the sight of me. I hear him coat himself with my saliva.

One of his hands grips my hair, the other my wrists, and his cock pushes against my asshole.

His lips find my ear. "I love you, but I need to punish you. Your lips are mine."

"You are such a bastard. You're just trying to find an excuse to fuck my ass," I say back.

His lips cover mine, but he doesn't kiss me. "You know I am." For a second, his face lightens as he winks at me, just for me, not for whoever could be spying on us from the dozens of ships nearby. Kai and Enzo have loyal employees, but I don't doubt that one of them is working for Julian or Bishop, and they're taking pictures to report.

When Zeke removes his face from mine, his eyes have darkened again. It looks likes he's taking from me, raping me, even though he's giving me everything he has. I know when we get to the privacy of the bedroom, he will kiss me sweetly and make me come with his tongue, but this is what is needed now. A show for Bishop. An angry fuck for us.

And then he pushes inside, squeezing his large cock inside my ass, stretching me so damn wide.

"No!" I scream, because it's fucking fun to pretend. Thankfully, Julian isn't in my head. The pain drove him from my mind.

My eyes water for real as he pushes into me, claiming me in a new way. But then one of his hands sneaks between my legs, one finger teasing my clit and another sliding into my pussy. It feels so incredibly delicious. I've never felt more connected to him, more like his than I do now.

"You like that, baby?" Zeke growls his voice torn between the truth and the lie.

"No," I strain back, my teeth tightly grinding together.

There is a flash of worry in Zeke's eyes, so I make mine extra wild to show I'm acting. We should have come up with a safeword.

His jaw ticks as he studies me, finally realizing the truth.

"I'm going to fuck you so hard you won't even dare look at another man."

I nod, and he makes good on his threat.

He fucks and thrusts and pushes so hard that I feel like I'm going to burst.

"I hate these damn names on your neck," Zeke says after a dozen thrusts.

He grabs a shard of glass and slices through my skin, making it look worse for the cameras, but I love him for crossing out the names, his included.

"You belong to yourself, but I hope you freely give yourself to me over and over."

"I do," I say, my finger twisting my wedding ring behind my back so Zeke can see.

And then we both come. His is a ferocious growl of taking what he wants. Mine is a cry of being claimed. Both are an act of love. An act I hope we repeat over and over again.

26

ZEKE

I DON'T KNOW HOW TO REACT WHEN I'M DONE FUCKING SIREN. I want to wrap her in my arms and never let her go. But that isn't what I should be doing for Bishop's little bitch of a spy watching us.

For him, I should spank Siren's ass and drag her kicking and screaming to my room. I don't want that kiss with Enzo to go to waste. I don't want anything to get in the way of Bishop fixing Siren. I need her whole. I need her brain clear of his thoughts and commands.

If Siren is going to listen to a man, I want it to be me, not that that is likely either. Siren will always be in control of her own life. I will always be chasing after her, hoping I'm enough for her.

But right now, I have to take the lead. So I grab one of Siren's wrists and yank her away from the piano. She tries to smooth her dress down, but I pull her tightly to my body until she is no longer thinking about her dress. She's only thinking about me.

Siren looks at me like I'm her whole world, and I smirk internally. *How did she trick me into so many lies for so long?*

She's horrible at this acting thing. It's plain as day that Siren is in love with me, even now.

Then, I'm pulling Siren down the stairs to our bedroom. I yank her inside and throw the door shut before kissing her hard against the door.

She gasps like I'm stealing all of her oxygen.

I moan like she's stealing all of my everything.

Her tongue slices through my mouth, and I know where this is headed, but we don't have time. We have to focus on our tasks at hand.

"Siren, baby, we can't," I moan, not believing that I'm turning down this woman.

She runs her hand through my hair, stroking my face. "I know."

But we don't stop. We kiss and kiss and kiss. I carry her to the shower, turning on the water to clean myself off before I fuck her.

And then, her legs are wrapped around me, my pants are shoved down to my ankles, her dress is hiked up to her waist, and I'm sliding between her wet folds.

"What are you doing to me?" I moan, my brain foggy and unable to remember the important task I should be doing.

"Showing you how good loving me can feel," she whispers back before grabbing my ass and pushing me all the way in.

Her ass felt nice, and it was a good excuse to fuck her there, but there is nothing like fucking her pussy, where I belong.

I fuck her under the water. There is a nice warm bed three feet away, but we never make it that far. We fuck here, in the shower, water beading down our bodies.

It feels like goodbye.

"This isn't goodbye," I grind into her, feeling all of her slickness, all of her tightness, all of her.

"I know," she whispers sadly. Her lips kiss mine tenderly.

I stop. "I'm not going to keep fucking you until I believe you."

Her eyes stop as she takes a deep breath. And then they are memorizing every part of my body. Every scar, every mark, every ripple of muscle. She's watching everything. Her hands move over where her eyes roamed, feeling everything so that if her eyes fail her, her fingers will remember.

I grab her hands. "Siren, stop."

"No, there is no guarantee of tomorrow. No guarantee of five seconds from now. No guarantee of forever."

"We promised forever."

"I know, but we don't get to decide how long our forever lasts. We don't get to know."

I kiss her hand. "That doesn't mean we should just give up."

"I'm not giving up; I'm making sure our forever lasts longer by taking it with me. No matter what separates us, this I will remember."

"Nothing is going to separate us." But it's a lie. I feel it to my bones. I know what we are both capable of doing for love. I know what is coming. I know what dangers are lurking just out our window. And I know this could be goodbye for now.

So I soak up everything about Siren too. Every curve, every line, every soft smile. I feel all of her warm skin. I remember every feminine smell.

I start moving, gliding in and out of her, and I memorize all of that too. I don't need to memorize how she looks or sounds when she comes. I already remember it all. This time will be like all the rest and become a part of me forever.

I try to stall as long as I can. I try to make our orgasms slow and stretch out the release we both want, but it's wishful thinking. There is no way to hold our orgasms back. Our bodies need them as much as we need our next breath. Our bodies will fall over the cliff whether I help us along or not.

I thrust again and we are both orgasming in a beautiful melody that has become our own song.

Just don't let our love fall. Those were the words she sang before. I never intend to. But somehow, when we both come down from our high, it feels like our love is falling down too.

"I need to go warn Kai that Bishop and Julian are coming, so we can put our plan into motion," I say.

"I'll be here," Siren responds.

I kiss her on the cheek, set her down, dry off, and get dressed. Siren heads into the closet with a towel around her body and comes out wearing jeans, a black shirt, and a thick leather jacket. I'm sure she's covered in knives and guns, ready for them to attack at any minute.

"You think they are going to attack tonight?" I ask. "Or are you planning on sleeping in leather?"

"I don't know when they are going to attack, but Bishop wants me to meet him at five in the morning."

I nod. "You aren't leaving this room, though. I'll come get you at five to meet Bishop. Promise me you won't fight unless the battle comes to you. You have our baby to protect."

"I won't leave this room until you come for me. I won't fight unless I have to."

"Thank you." I walk over to her, then lean down and

kiss her stomach, where I still can't believe she's growing our baby.

"Go," Siren says, basically pushing me out the door to get me to leave.

Once outside the door, I process what just happened. *Did I just say goodbye to Siren? Is the battle really starting now?*

Fuck, I need to find Kai and get ready.

I don't know where Kai went. She said she was going to another yacht, but I know her. She didn't go anywhere. I wander around on the yacht, not finding any sign of her. I know she didn't go back to bed. And then I spot Enzo, sitting on the edge of one of the decks looking out at the ocean.

I'm not ready to forgive him. I know why Siren seduced him, tricked him, whatever the hell happened. But he let it happen. He didn't know she was doing it to try and get her life back. He let her kiss him, knowing how deeply that knife would hurt all of us.

But I don't want him dead. Tomorrow, I can forgive him. Today, I just want him fighting by me, alive.

"They're coming," I say, giving him a tight look.

He nods. He doesn't ask for forgiveness. He just cracks his neck and then reaches for the gun on him, holding it close.

"Where is she?" I ask.

He nods forward. He's watching Kai from afar, ensuring her safety while giving her the space she needs.

I doubt she'll want to talk to me either, but she doesn't have a choice.

I hop down onto the lower deck and find Kai sitting with her feet dangling over the edge as she leans back against the railing. One wrong move could send her into the ocean below. She has a lit cigar in her hand, but she's not smoking it, just smelling it.

I sigh. Of course, she has to be sitting on the edge of the yacht, where my big ass is going to struggle to sit.

I walk over, and I know she can sense me. "Any chance you want to climb on this side of the railing for this talk, Stingray?"

"No way in hell. Your stupid ass plan is why I'm sitting here in the first place," Kai says.

I laugh and then take my time climbing over the railing. I grip it as I sink down until I'm sitting next to her. I loop my arms through the railing behind me as my ass doesn't fit on the tiny lip Kai is sitting on.

"It wasn't my plan," I say.

She laughs manically. "Don't lie to me, Zeke. I know that plan had something to do with helping Siren. It was something Bishop wanted her to do. Something that would save her. I'm not mad at you for doing it, but don't lie to me and say you didn't know. That's why you went with me to prepare all the men for war."

I sigh. "Yes, I knew Siren was going to do something Bishop wanted. But I didn't realize it had anything to do with Enzo and definitely didn't know it involved kissing him."

She shakes her head. "You would have let them kiss again if it meant saving Siren."

"I guess."

She sniffs one of Enzo's cigars. "I'm not ready to forgive him, or you, or her. I know it was just a kiss, but in this world, we face so many dangers. I just thought I'd never have to worry about Enzo's loyalty. I never thought I'd be faced with him kissing another woman with her hand in his pants. I never thought that was even a worry I needed to have. I thought our relationship was invincible."

"It is. You don't have to worry about Enzo's loyalties. Siren tricked him. That's kind of one of her main skill sets," I say.

"It doesn't matter. He still kissed her."

"No, she kissed him against his will. She manipulated us as much as she did Enzo. She made you believe he was willing; he wasn't."

Kai looks out at the dark ocean, several yachts visible just as dots in the distance.

"You don't have to forgive Siren, or me for my part in all of this. But you do need to forgive Enzo, just not until after tomorrow."

"Why?"

"Because you love him."

Kai shakes her head. "No, I mean, why not until tomorrow?"

"Because they are coming. The battle is here. In the next couple of hours, for sure by morning. They think we are fighting. They think we are weak. Let them think that."

I reach over and give her hand a tight squeeze. "Don't let this affect you, Stingray. The kiss meant nothing."

"You forgave her already, didn't you?"

I nod. "Our lives are too short not to forgive. It doesn't matter what she does. I'm not saying I would stay with her if she changed, if she started abusing me or something. But I will forgive her when she makes a mistake, especially one she did to save my child from herself."

I climb back over the railing.

"Alaska," Kai says, giving me a knowing look, telling me where the box is. She trusts me, and now I carry the burden of knowing too. "I don't forgive you or Siren because there is nothing to forgive. I would kill you all if I had to in order to protect my kids. I don't fault you for doing the same thing."

I nod, and start heading back to Siren, for a few last moments together.

I see the shadow before I hear him. He's here. On the ship. Trying to sneak around in the night.

"We need to talk. We can end this war before it even starts," Julian says. *Don't talk, kill him.*

I turn and fire.

27

SIREN

I hear the fire of a gun, and I know Zeke isn't coming back. The battle has started, and I'm stuck here feeling useless until it ends.

It's two in the morning, three hours until Bishop told me to meet him to undo what he fucked up in my head. *What if he's killed before then? What if Zeke is?*

I can't think. I need to shut my brain down. I need to disappear inside myself. I need to focus on finding a way to fight Bishop off from within. That's the way to ensure our victory—by not needing Bishop to fix me in the first place.

But it's not just Bishop I have to worry about.

It's Julian.

And Bishop.

And even Zeke.

All three men have tried to control me. All men have the power to manipulate me.

Julian Reed has taken so much from me, but his power is now limited. He's already used his threat against me, so I know how bad it can get.

Bishop is just getting started, but I have a secret of my

own where he is concerned. But that secret will destroy more than just me.

And Zeke Kane is a monster, my monster. He has so much grit and raw manliness inside him. So much darkness that he's always flittering between right and wrong. So far, he's always ended up on the side of good, *but will that always be the case?*

I hear all the men's voices in my head, and I realize Bishop isn't the only one who can control me in this way.

"You're mine," Julian says.

"You're mine," Bishop says.

"You're mine," Zeke says.

But I only want to be one man's.

"Do you? I thought you were a more independent woman than that, Siren? Why should any man own you at all?" Bishop asks in my head.

"No, don't you start. You don't care about me, you just want me to be loyal to you," I say.

"No, I want you to be loyal to yourself. Once you are, the commands I put in your head you will do willingly," Bishop continues.

Fuck.

No.

Stop thinking, Siren. Focus on the sounds. The gunfire. The bombs. The muffled sounds from this soundproof room.

Fuck, why did I promise Zeke I would stay in this room?

Why?

Why?

Why?

If Bishop wasn't already in my head, if Julian wasn't already haunting my dreams, I would think I'm going crazy.

I know what crazy looks like, and fearing for everyone I love isn't it.

Yet, I feel myself going mad while I wait for Zeke to come to me. Waiting has never been my strong suit, but I made a promise. I grip my shirt over my stomach; it's not just me I have to worry about anymore.

So I sit on the edge of the bed and stare at the door—praying that it opens to a smiling Zeke.

Instead, I hear multiple men outside. I move to the security camera screen that points out to the door. I watch the men place something against the door, and then step back.

A bomb.

I stare at the camera—a five minute timer starts on the bomb. That's how long I have left in my prison. It's how long I have left to live. Zeke could save me—he could save us. *But at what cost?*

28

ZEKE

"You missed. I thought you had better aim than that, boy," Julian says.

I frown. *What is it about this guy that I just can't kill him?*

Something deeper is holding me back. Something deep down is preventing me from killing him. *Something...*

"Why can't I kill you?" I ask, not meaning to admit that out loud, but saying it all the same.

Julian snickers. "You haven't figured it out yet?"

I frown. *How should I know?* I never miss. When I shoot, I kill. But with Julian, even when I'm aiming, I miss.

"Don't worry, your wife figured it out," Julian says.

I freeze. *How does he know?*

"I spotted your wedding ring. I assume there is a reason you are wearing it," Julian says.

"What do you want?"

"Just to let you know, I'll blow up your wife's bedroom if you don't hear me out. You and I have a deal, after all. One that you keep trying to run away from," Julian says, holding up his phone, showing me a picture of Siren's room with explosives on the door.

I feel the yacht jolt forward. I'm sure it's Julian's doing, trying to separate us from our fleet of men.

I growl, my anger palpating through me as I keep the gun aimed at Julian's head. "Don't touch her."

"I don't plan to. I have other, more important things, to get from you."

"Like?"

"You owe me two more sins or truths. But since you'll never tell me the truth, you can commit a sin," Julian says.

I frown, not liking this.

"Retrieve the box," Julian says, looking past me. I feel more people gathering around us on the main deck, and I don't have to look to know who is standing behind me—Kai and Enzo. Kai is to my left, Enzo my right.

"Welcome, everyone," Julian says.

I swallow.

"You're not getting away, not this time," Kai says.

"You thought your little games could break us up, not going to happen. We fight together," Enzo says.

"I'm always up for a good fight with my friends," Langston says.

Langston's voice gets me to turn. He's standing next to Enzo. He looks good, although a bit worn down and unshaven. He winks at me when I turn.

I exhale a breath. Everyone who needs to be here is here. We can figure out how to take him down, then hunt down Bishop and do the same to him. This time, they will all end up dead. We all point our guns at Julian.

"It's over. Let Siren go, and we'll make your death quick," I say.

Julian laughs. "I won't be the one dying tonight. But if I do, Siren will die at the same time."

I stiffen. He's holding his phone, showing a countdown until the bomb detonates.

I can't kill him until the bomb is disarmed.

"Go," I say to Langston.

And then he's gone to hopefully disarm the bomb in time.

Julian looks at his watch. "He has three minutes. Do you think he's fast enough? Because if I don't enter in the code by then, the bomb will go off."

"What do you want?"

"You have two sins left. Finish them, and I won't harm Siren. Finish them, and I'll let her live."

Julian is careful with his words. He doesn't promise me my life, just hers—it's enough. He knows that. He knows all I care about is making sure that she lives, that our baby lives.

"These last two sins are different than the rest—darker, more dangerous. Requiring more loyalty than you've given me so far," Julian's eyes seer.

Hurry up, Langston. I need Siren safe.

"Whatever it is, I'll do it," I say, no words I've ever spoken have been truer.

Julian nods. "Prove it."

"How?"

I cringe, knowing Kai and Enzo need to run because whatever he's going to have me do involves them.

"Kill Enzo," Julian says.

This is about loyalty. And time is ticking down. I turn and shoot, not giving Enzo or myself time to think. I aim for the shoulder, hoping it's enough to appease Julian.

Julian laughs as Kai shrieks.

"What's the final sin?" I ask, knowing we've already

wasted a minute. I only have two minutes left to get this madman to turn off the bomb.

"That wasn't your sin. Just the test. And you failed."

"I shot him."

"I said *kill* him."

"If I kill him, that completes one of my two sins," I say, trying to come up with a way to save Enzo and Siren. An idea forms in my head for how to save Enzo. I don't love it, but it gives him a fighting chance.

Julian looks behind me. "Fine, kill Enzo Black, the leader of the great Black empire, and you'll only have one sin left."

I turn and look at Kai's pleading eyes as she holds onto the wound in Enzo's shoulder.

"Disarm the bomb, Julian," I say.

"Not until Enzo is dead."

A tear waters my eyes, knowing what I'm about to do. I turn, counting down my final sixty seconds that I have to do something until Siren dies. Julian will kill her this time if I don't do this, but I'm hoping Langston found a way to stop this before I get to her.

Sixty.

Fifty-nine.

Fifty-eight.

I walk over to Kai, who is leaning over Enzo's body. I look at her, searching her eyes for any solution that she has. She wants to fight. To shoot Julian and call his bluff. We were supposed to shoot him and Bishop the second we saw them. Well, Bishop isn't showing himself, and Julian, as always, is one step ahead of us.

Fifty.

Forty-nine.

Forty-eight.

I look down at Enzo, who gives me a tight nod avoiding his wife, knowing she's not going to let me do what I'm about to do easily. If she's pissed at Siren for kissing Enzo, she sure as hell will never speak to me again if I kill him.

Thirty.

Twenty-nine.

Twenty-eight.

"I'm sorry," I whisper to them both. I used to think I would never betray them. I would never choose anyone else above them. I was wrong.

Siren and our baby are the only things that matter to me. I'll save Kai and Enzo the best I can, but if I have to trade their lives to save Siren's and my baby, I will.

With a swift punch, I knock Kai back onto her ass, hitting her hard enough to temporarily knock her unconscious. I raise my gun and fire into Enzo, ensuring plenty of blood loss and show for Julian as I hit him in the gut. I pray I don't hit any vital organs.

Enzo growls as his eyes go to his wife, who is knocked out cold behind me.

"Bastard," Enzo curses, already weak from blood loss but still caring more about his wife than he does himself. If I survive this fight with Julian, Enzo will kill me himself. Even if Enzo doesn't survive this, he'll come back as a ghost to kill me.

I grab Enzo's hand and pull him to the edge of the yacht.

Twenty.

Nineteen.

Eighteen.

"We always said we'd die for those we love," I say.

Enzo nods. I push his almost lifeless body into the fast ocean current, much like when I was shot on his yacht and fell into the ocean. I was left to die. To drown.

I was inches away from death before Siren found me. I just hope Enzo doesn't have to wait as long as I did to be found.

Fifteen.

Fourteen.

Thirteen.

"Enzo's dead. Now disarm the bomb. Let Siren go."

Julian tsks. "He's not dead."

"Yet," I finish. "He's not dead yet, but I thought you'd prefer the great Enzo Black to suffer a long, torturous death. That's the death he deserves, not a clean bullet to the heart."

Ten.

Nine.

Eight.

God, please work. If I have to shoot Enzo in the head, though, I will. Just please don't make me.

Julian lifts his phone, considering.

Five.

Four.

Three.

Julian types in a code and then shows me the phone.

I exhale. He disarmed the bomb. Siren's safe.

"Now, where is the box? Get me to the box and unlock it, and I'll never lay a hand on Siren again," Julian says.

"Alaska, the box is in Alaska," I say, grateful that Kai told me a location, so I could use it now to save my wife.

Kai sits up, now wide awake. She glares at me as she dives overboard, racing to find Enzo.

"You're going to take me to Alaska and lead me to that box."

"I will," I say, betraying everyone but Siren. This is why I shouldn't have fallen in love.

Siren is my everything. I just ruined years of friendships. I possibly ended my friend's life. Siren tried to destroy a marriage. All to protect our own love.

I just chose a side. I chose Julian's. I am no longer loyal to the Black name. I'll do whatever Julian or Bishop want in order to protect Siren and my baby.

Julian ensured my loyalty, and I've never hated myself more.

"I'll take you to the box. I'll be loyal to you. But Siren stays here under Langton's protection. And if you lay a finger on her again, you'll wish you were dead."

Julian nods as I march downstairs.

I'm devastated by what I did, and even more wrecked by what I'm about to do.

29

SIREN

I'M USUALLY A FIGHTER.

When I'm put in a horrible situation, I fight. But this time, I sit silently. I meditate, I pray, I hope.

I don't pray for myself.

I don't meditate for Zeke.

I hope that when we both die, this life inside me finds a way to live, to forgive us for not being enough.

The only way we save each other and this baby is by burning every city, every friend, every person to the ground. We turn them all to ash. Our love is too big. Our sins too great. We were never meant to love each other. I was wrong —I thought finding Zeke in that vast ocean was fate.

I thought it meant that we were meant to be.

That our love was supposed to find each other.

But it wasn't fate.

It wasn't destiny.

It was the devil taking a stab in the dark and pushing two people who have just enough darkness in their hearts together and then sitting back and watching the carnage they would inflict evolve.

I may not be able to see the future, but I can see ours. It ends in destruction—of us or our friends.

We've chosen us.

Over and over again.

It leaves us alone and in pain. Sure, we have each other. We love each other. *But is that enough? Is our love enough to survive on?*

No.

But if we choose our friends, can we live without love?

No.

We are at an impasse. We should have never found each other. We should have never have created this life.

I wait, trying to figure out which option Zeke chose—us or them.

I wait for the bomb or the quiet.

The door unlocks, and Zeke appears. He chose us.

My eyes water, not able to imagine the destruction he just caused and is yet to cause.

"I have to go," he says.

I nod, unable to speak, but agreeing. I break.

"I know," Zeke says, knowing what's already in my heart. "I know, Siren, I know."

He steps closer.

"I'm sorry," I say, breaking more inside.

"I'm not." He lifts me until we are both standing together.

"Our love was never meant to last forever," Zeke says, his own tears dripping down onto our joined hands.

"But we promised. We vowed. We loved—forever," I say, my words broken and painful.

"We kept those promises," Zeke says.

We kiss. One last kiss to last the lifetime never meant to be.

Our rings touch, rings that represent a marriage that was never real. One that was only ever real to us.

He walks toward the door, and it's then that I realize I don't know the truth anymore. I don't know if he's doing this on his own accord or because Julian demands it. *I don't know if this is a truth, a lie, or a sin?*

I'll find out, though. If there is a chance this is all a sin, then I still have a chance at my happily ever after.

Tears are falling fast now, so painful and real they wreck my entire body, shaking me until I can barely stand.

"I have to go, but you'll be safe—always and forever. Nothing will ever change that." Zeke moves his head, and then he's pushing a man inside my room. "This is my best friend, Langston. He'll protect you, no matter what."

I freeze.

I can't think.

I don't hear the rest of Zeke's words.

I can't process them.

I can't believe what is happening.

I can't believe what I'm seeing.

I can't...

I try to find Zeke. I try to find the words to tell him. To explain to him what is happening. But I can't.

I fucking can't.

By the time I do, Zeke is gone. All that is left is Langston —a man I know very well.

A man who isn't Langston at all.

Langston is dead, at least, his soul is.

Langston is the man who has been haunting my dreams.

He's the man who can control my thoughts.

Bishop—Langston Bishop—my own personal nightmare.

I run to the door and try to get past him. Zeke couldn't have gone far.

But Langston Bishop grabs me as I try to move past.

"Zeke!" I yell and cry. He either doesn't hear my call or chooses not to listen.

My entire body trembles with fear and pain. I'm having a panic attack. I can't breathe, as Bishop throws me on the bed.

"Zeke's gone. You're finally free. Free of love, of pain," Bishop says.

I don't feel free at all, though. I feel loss. Zeke just sacrificed everything and left me alone with the one man who hijacked my mind.

My eyes widen at the thought of everything else we're about to lose.

The End

Thank you so much for reading! Zeke and Siren's story concludes in Broken Anchor

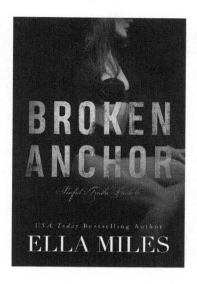

Grab the entire Sinful Truths series below!
Sinful Truth #1
Twisted Vow #2
Reckless Fall #3
Tangled Promise #4
Fallen Love #5
Broken Anchor #6

Read Enzo and Kai's story below in the Truth or Lies series!
(You also get to read Zeke's beginning)
Taken by Lies #1
Betrayed by Truths #2
Trapped by Lies #3
Stolen by Truths #4
Possessed by Lies #5
Consumed by Truths #6

FREE BOOKS

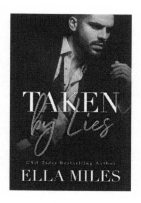

Read **Taken by Lies** for **FREE**! And sign up to get my latest releases, updates, and more goodies here→EllaMiles.com/freebooks

Follow me on **BookBub** to get notified of my new releases and recommendations here→Follow on BookBub Here

Join **Ella's Bellas FB group** to get **Pretend I'm Yours** for **FREE**→Join Ella's Bellas Here

ORDER SIGNED PAPERBACKS

I love putting my signed paperbacks on SALE!

Check them out by visiting my website:
https://ellamiles.com/signed-paperbacks

ALSO BY ELLA MILES

SINFUL TRUTHS:

TRUTH OR LIES:

DIRTY SERIES:

Dirty Revenge

Dirty: The Complete Series

ALIGNED SERIES:

Aligned: Volume 1 (Free Series Starter)

Aligned: Volume 2

Aligned: Volume 3

Aligned: Volume 4

Aligned: The Complete Series Boxset

UNFORGIVABLE SERIES:

Heart of a Thief

Heart of a Liar

Heart of a Prick

Unforgivable: The Complete Series Boxset

MAYBE, DEFINITELY SERIES:

Maybe Yes

Maybe Never

Maybe Always

Definitely Yes

Definitely No

Definitely Forever

STANDALONES:

Pretend I'm Yours

Finding Perfect

Savage Love

Too Much

Not Sorry

ABOUT THE AUTHOR

Ella Miles writes steamy romance, including everything from dark suspense romance that will leave you on the edge of your seat to contemporary romance that will leave you laughing out loud or crying. Most importantly, she wants you to feel everything her characters feel as you read.

Ella is currently living her own happily ever after near the Rocky Mountains with her high school sweetheart husband. Her heart is also taken by her goofy five year old black lab who is scared of everything, including her own shadow.

Ella is a USA Today Bestselling Author & Top 50 Bestselling Author.

Stalk Ella at:
www.ellamiles.com
ella@ellamiles.com

Made in the USA
Columbia, SC
25 July 2022